PRAISE FOR REBEKAH CRANE

The Upside of Falling Down

"[An] appealing love story that provides romantics with many swoon-worthy moments."

—*Publishers Weekly*

"Written with [an] unstoppable mix of sharp humor, detailed characters, and all-around charm, this story delivers a fresh and enticing take on first love—and one that will leave readers swooning."

—Jessica Park, author of *180 Seconds* and *Flat-Out Love*

"*The Upside of Falling Down* is a romantic new-adult celebration of all of the wild and amazing possibilities that open up when perfect plans go awry."

—*Foreword Magazine*

"Using the device of Clementine's amnesia, Crane explores themes of freedom and self-determination . . . readers will respond to [Clementine's] testing of new waters. A light exploration of existential themes."

—*Kirkus Reviews*

"Crane's contemporary YA offers a light take on heavy issues . . . readers who enjoy a charming Irish setting with a sweet romance and brooding hero may want to pick this one up."

—RT Book Reviews

"[R]eaders glimpse a new side of Ireland. Clementine is a resilient heroine . . . the book ultimately rewards . . ."

—Booklist Online

"This quickly paced work will be enjoyed by teens interested in independence, love, self-discovery, and drama."

—*School Library Journal*

"First love, starting over, finding herself—the story is hopeful and romantic."

—*Denver Life*

The Odds of Loving Grover Cleveland

"Now that the title has captured our attention, I have even better news: No, this book isn't a history lesson about a president. Much more wonderfully, it centers on teenager Zander Osborne, who meets a boy named Grover Cleveland at a camp for at-risk youth. Together, the two and other kids who face bipolar disorder, anorexia, pathological lying, schizophrenia, and other obstacles use their group therapy sessions to break down and build themselves back up. And as Zander gets closer to Grover, she wonders if happiness is actually a possibility for her after all."

—Bustle

"The true beauty of Crane's book lies in the way she handles the ugly, painful details of real life, showing the glimmering humanity beneath the façades of even her most troubled characters. Crane shows, with enormous heart and wisdom, how even the unlikeliest of friendships can give us the strength we need to keep on fighting."

—RT Book Reviews

THE INFINITE PIECES OF US

ALSO BY REBEKAH CRANE

The Upside of Falling Down
The Odds of Loving Grover Cleveland
Aspen
Playing Nice

THE INFINITE PIECES OF US

REBEKAH CRANE

SKYSCAPE

SKYSCAPE

This is a work of fiction. Names, characters, organizations, places, events, and incidents are either products of the author's imagination or are used fictitiously. Any resemblance to actual persons, living or dead, or actual events is purely coincidental.

Text copyright © 2018 by Rebekah Crane
All rights reserved.

Published by Skyscape, New York

www.apub.com

Amazon, the Amazon logo, and Skyscape are trademarks of Amazon.com, Inc., or its affiliates.

ISBN-13: 9781503903951 (hardcover)
ISBN-10: 1503903958 (hardcover)
ISBN-13: 9781503903968 (paperback)
ISBN-10: 1503903966 (paperback)

Cover design by Liz Casal

Printed in the United States of America

First Edition

For my dad—who never tires of the numinous.
And for Renee—who never tired of this book. It exists
because of you.

IN THE BEGINNING THERE WAS . . .

A pool. It's an empty pool. I guess all things are nothing at the start. Mom, Tom, Hannah, and I stand on the edge of the pool at our new house, looking down into the nothingness.

"I promised you a pool," Tom says enthusiastically.

"But it's empty," Hannah says.

The sun is setting and a few stars twinkle in the twilight. I didn't know the sky could be this big. "And my lips are chapped," she adds.

"You need to drink more water," Mom says.

I look at the chipped paint at the bottom of the pool. The pool is chapped. It needs water, too.

"Look on the bright side," Tom says. "We have a pool, and one day we might fill it."

Is that what this is? Is *this* the bright side?

"I'm going to unpack." Hannah walks away.

"Me, too." Mom follows.

Tom looks at me. "Don't fall in." He walks away, too.

I climb down the ladder into the empty pool and lie on the cracked, dry floor. I put my hands behind my head and tell myself, *I won't drown.*

There isn't enough water in the desert to drown.

After a while, I hear Mom yelling from inside the house. "Esther, where'd you go?"

Esther, where'd you go? I ask the stars.

They don't answer me. I don't expect them to. Answers don't come that easily.

1

Our house smells like warm, lifeless air. The walls are made of sand. The people who lived here before us painted the entire house beige. Like sand. It's like they're covering the sand with something that looks like sand.

Tom likes the neutral color because it matches everything. I think Tom wants to pretend that he's neutral and boring, when we all know he's covering a snake tattoo on his forearm that he got when he wasn't neutral and boring. But he was also on a lot of drugs at that time in his life, so Mom says we're not allowed to bring it up. Ever.

It's a cobra with fangs. I've only seen it a few times when I've caught him wearing an undershirt in the bathroom. The snake coils around his forearm all the way down to his wrist. He wears long sleeves every day, even when it's over one hundred degrees, to cover it up. But every now and then, I'll catch a glimpse of the tail. It's weird to see it. Almost like I'm catching him naked.

Mom likes to remind Hannah and me that Tom didn't get to grow up like we will—with *two* loving parents. I thought we were doing just fine with one. I understand that one plus one equals two, and two is more than one. My math skills far outreach addition. But more doesn't always equal love.

Which brings me back to our house that is unwelcoming, so much so that it feels heartless, like it didn't care who moved in and never will.

It's also full of the crap we moved from Ohio to New Mexico, but it feels empty. And yet, this house is twice the size of our old house.

> Complex Math Problem: If all things are matter, and matter takes up space, and space weighs something, why does Esther's new house feel so empty even though it's filled with crap?

There's a cactus outside my bedroom window that's drinking up all the water in the desert. The cactus thrives while I have chapped lips. It's a selfish cactus, which I guess is the nature of a cactus. It's built to suck up water. I can't blame it for doing what nature intended it to do.

In truth, though, I wish I could chop it down.

But since it's so prickly, no one can touch it. I suddenly feel bad for the cactus, because it didn't choose to be this way. It just *is* this way. And then I think I shouldn't be so hard on my sister, Hannah.

Mom comes into my room with a new water bottle and a dress. I'm supposed to be unpacking, but I don't know where to start.

Mom holds out the dress. "I found it at the store today."

The dress is clearly a medium, and the water bottle has my name written down the side. "Thanks," I say.

Mom looks at all the boxes and draws out a long exhale. "It should fit by Christmas."

She's talking about the dress, but really I think she means this house.

"It's strange to live in a place where people wear cowboy boots for real," Mom says.

I look at the water bottle. "Why not just use a glass?"

Mom moans a little at my question. "You can keep track of how much you're drinking. People get dehydrated all the time out here."

That's because this place is a raisin. It doesn't get dehydrated—it *is* dehydrated.

She gets up and walks out of my bedroom, adding, "Why don't you go ride your bike or something? That's what people do in this town. It'll help, and we'll fit in."

I hang my new dress in my spacious and empty closet. Mom said it will fit by Christmas, but it's a summer dress with flowers on it and too much white for its own good.

I look at the cactus right outside my window and take a drink from my water bottle.

"Are you jealous?" I ask it.

But even the cactus knows better than to be jealous of me.

∞

At dinner, over a plate of baked chicken and steamed peas, Mom makes a suggestion.

"Let's get a dog," she says, poking at her peas. "Everyone has dogs here."

"No," Tom says.

"Why not?"

"They're too messy."

Tom has a thing about messes. He can't stand them.

"I'm with Tom," Hannah says.

"But they keep the coyotes away," Mom says, sticking the peas so hard that a few fall on the ground. Tom groans and bends over to pick them up. "See, if we had a dog, the dog would just eat the mess."

"Let's try not to make the mess in the first place." Tom places the peas next to his plate.

"Wait. Are there coyotes here?" Hannah says.

"There are coyotes in Ohio, too," I say. Hannah visually assaults me.

"This meal is bland. I need ketchup." Hannah gets an armful of condiments from the fridge and sets them on the table. I reach for the mayonnaise, and Mom shakes her head.

"Is God real?" I ask. I know I shouldn't, but they know I ask questions I shouldn't ask.

Mom, Tom, and Hannah stare at me. Hannah shakes the ketchup bottle forcefully and squeezes a glob onto her plate. No one answers. It's a dinnertime standoff—who can ignore what Esther just said the longest.

Mom breaks first. "Well, if we can't get a dog, we need some friends."

"We've only been here a week," Tom says.

"No better time to get started." Mom fills up everyone's water bottles. "Now, drink up . . ." And then she looks at me, which makes Tom look at me, which makes Hannah do the same. "So we can avoid having any more problems around here."

2

Tom hires Happy Houses Cleaning Company to come every Tuesday because "a clean house is a happy home." That's the company's motto, and Tom is desperate for our house to become a home. We've been here two weeks now. So far the house still feels heartless, even though Mom bought a light fixture with antlers and a sign for our front door that says **HOWDY! NOW, WIPE YOUR BOOTS!** She's trying to fit in.

> Complex Math Problem: How do you solve the messes
> you can't see? In other words—Is fitting in just covering
> up who you really are in hopes that people don't notice?

Mom, Hannah, and I are going through boxes of winter clothes in the living room to donate to charity and unclutter the house. The hats, gloves, snow pants, and jackets are piled up high. I feel like I could jump into the center of the pile and smell snow.

But it's almost one hundred degrees today.

I put on one of the hats with a big furry ball on the top. "Does it ever get cold enough to snow in southern New Mexico?"

"Who cares," Hannah says. She takes the hat off my head. The static generated from the cotton and dry air rubbing against my head makes my short brown hair stand on end. "You look like a boy when you wear hats."

Hannah takes the box of winter gear marked for Goodwill and sets it by the front door for later. Mom tells us to finish unpacking our rooms for the cleaning company, to which I promptly reply, "But isn't it their job to clean?"

"Don't be a snob, Esther," Mom says.

But I didn't mean to be a snob. It was a genuine question. Hannah rolls her eyes. She doesn't need to clean her room because she already put everything away the first day we moved in. Hannah's just that way. She doesn't like a mess any more than Tom does, which is probably why Tom lets Hannah get away with stuff. He assumes she'll always clean up after herself, so we won't have to. But really good murderers clean up after themselves, too, so they don't get caught.

I could never be a murderer. My room is a mess. Clothes are everywhere. Mom keeps telling me to go through them and find what fits and what doesn't, but that would mean trying things on. Stepping back into old clothes will lead to the road Mom doesn't want me to go down again, a road she's trying to cover with cowboy boots and antlers and Mexican blankets that don't match our couches, which still smell like Ohio—like rain and mud and lake water.

And I'm trying to be better this time.

I am no longer a whole number. I carry a decimal now. Each box in my room is just a reminder of my remainder. The problem is, I can't figure out if I'm less than or more than I was before. I know I'm not the same.

I sit down on my bed and work on math homework instead. When it seems like there are too many questions that will remain unanswered, math is my solve-ation. Tom would prefer me to find salvation in Jesus, but that seems really hard. With math, a question doesn't exist without an answer. It's a guarantee. If I work on a problem long enough, I *will* solve it.

Complex Math Problem: What happens when I find a math problem that I can't solve?

∞

When a vacuum cleaner pushes my bedroom door open, I wake up startled. Happy Houses Cleaning Company. Right.

I yawn, rubbing my eyes, then stand up quickly, ready to clean my room yet paralyzed as to where to start. I fumble around, moving this and that out of the way but not really doing anything. I'm just shifting things into new places.

"I'm sorry for the mess."

The person pushing the vacuum pulls earbuds from her ears. "What?" she yells.

"It's a mess!" I yell back.

"That's why I'm here!" she hollers with a smile. She puts the earbuds back in her ears and bobs her head as she vacuums. Curly red hair circles her head in what looks like a halo. It contrasts with her brown skin— she's fair *and* dark, combined into one.

She hums as she cleans, like maybe this isn't the worst job on the planet, even though I'm pretty sure it's close. Other people's bathrooms. Gross. Then I feel bad for the mess I've left. She has to work around all of it.

I tap her on the shoulder, and she pulls her earbuds out again, looking at me with inquisitive gray eyes. She's younger than I thought.

"Any suggestions on how to deal with this mess?" I ask, since she's the professional.

She shakes her head. "I just vacuum."

"Any chance you have the world's largest vacuum in your car?" I ask.

She laughs. "You're funny."

I can't help myself. "Want to hear a joke?"

"Sure."

"What do you get when you cross an algebra class with the prom?" I ask.

"What?" she says.

"The quadratic formal."

I know I shouldn't say it. The joke echoes of the past, linking me to a time Tom wishes never existed. But when she laughs, the air in the room starts to smell like warm, clear sunshine.

Maybe her vacuum works better than she thinks.

∞

I'm lying in the empty pool again after trying to clean my room. The box I opened contained my lucky rabbit's foot.

"It will bring you luck," he said. "And I know you need a miracle, but maybe luck is a miracle wrapped in different letters."

The memory of his voice stopped me from breathing, so I came out here. I think I'll sleep out here tonight. I can't sleep in my room anyway.

As I lie here with my eyes closed, our old, rusty trampoline from back in Ohio comes to mind. I see Mom, Hannah, and me sleeping out there all night. When one person shifted, all three of us would shift. We woke up in the morning, huddled into a ball of warm bodies, legs and arms intertwined.

"I wish we could bring it with us," Mom said when we left.

I wasn't sure if she meant the trampoline or the memory.

Why was the student afraid of the y-intercept? I ask myself.

"Why?" Amit said. I can actually hear his voice humming through the bare trees. It wants to get tangled in leaves, but in the desert, even the trees have to let go of whatever can't survive.

"She thought she'd be stung by the *B*." I whisper the answer to the wind.

I think it laughs.

"One more question," I say out loud. Or I think I say it out loud. But the truth is, it's as much inside of me as it is outside of me, all around me.

"Will this ever go away?" I ask the wind, hoping it will carry my question all the way back to Ohio. But I don't wait for a response. I know the wind doesn't blow backward, and Mom says I need to start moving forward.

∞

An alarming scream comes from inside the house. I climb up the pool ladder—not realizing in my haste that it would have been easier just to use the steps—but it still feels like I'm swimming in a pool, even though it's empty.

I run through the house, following the screams, to find Hannah holding the vacuum girl by the T-shirt. The girl is totally shocked, like a cat being held up by the scruff of the neck.

Mom bursts into the living room at the same time. "What's going on?"

The vacuum girl doesn't talk. I look at her, and she looks at me, and I think, *Hannah has held me like that before, too.* Figuratively, not physically.

"She was trying to steal our stuff," Hannah says, pointing to the box of winter items for Goodwill. "I caught her klepto hands all over it."

"Is that true?" Mom asks the girl, who looks around like she's caught in a trap.

But we are *giving* this stuff away. It was sitting at the door, practically homeless. You can't steal something from someone who doesn't own it anymore. Our house in Ohio wasn't *stolen* by a nice retired couple.

"I told her she could have it," I say. Mom and Hannah look at me, surprised. "I gave it to her. It's going to Goodwill anyway. I didn't think you'd mind."

"Oh," Mom says. She swats at Hannah. "Let go of her shirt. She's not a criminal. You're so dramatic sometimes."

The girl hesitates, looking down at the box and back at me, and then at Hannah, whose arms are hooked like a vise across her chest.

"Go on," I say, nudging her to play along with this awkward scene, as if we had already discussed it. Who's the dramatic one? "Take it."

The girl picks up the box, a little hesitantly, and says, "Thanks." She heads for the front door.

"You're welcome," I say. "Glad you can use it."

Hannah huffs away.

"We'll see you next week," Mom says as she closes the door.

Maybe by next week I'll have my mess cleaned up, but probably not. I hope the girl brings a strong vacuum again.

3

A gigantic replica of Jesus from the waist up sprouts from the front lawn of First Community Church of the Covenant Bible Fellowship of Truth or Consequences, New Mexico. It looks like Jesus is being born into the world again from beneath the ground. His arms rise high in the air, like a football referee signaling a touchdown. *He* is the reason we moved here—Touchdown Jesus. I've started calling the church Touchdown Church. It's easier to remember.

Tom saw an article, in one of his Christian magazines, about the gigantic statue and the youth pastor who had it erected. Pastor Rick says he was drawn to Truth or Consequences because even the name spoke the glory of God. He calls the gigantic Jesus statue the Lux Mundi, the Light of the World. When Tom read all this, he knew we needed to be a part of it. The conversation went something like this:

Tom: We should move to Truth or Consequences, New Mexico.

Mom: Is that a real place?

Tom (staring at me): A real place, and a good reminder. You need to live in the truth of the Lord or deal with the consequences.

Now we live in the town that changed its name in 1950 from Hot Springs to Truth or Consequences, after a game show. Apparently, people came on the show to answer a trivia question. If they answered wrong, they suffered some embarrassing consequence.

After the first Sunday we attended church here, I had a nightmare about the statue. I haven't gone close to Jesus since.

Here are a few other notable things about Pastor Rick. His last name is Wonder. He is young and gorgeous. His light-brown hair is always perfectly tousled, with just enough gel in it to look like slightly greasy bed head. His hooded sweatshirt smells like a mix of motor oil and coffee, and his beard is more scruff than actual beard. He loves Jesus and the word "awesome."

He is effortless.

Hannah and I joined the church choir in an attempt to "make friends." Plus, Hannah heard that every spring, the church puts on the musical *The Passion*, and she's determined to play Mary—because she's dramatic. We practice on Wednesdays, which means Wednesday is also the day we get to see Rick Wonder.

When he walks into the choir room, we stop midsong and stare. Even the boys. He's that good-looking. The only person completely unaware that Rick Wonder is among us is Beth, who sits beside me and always wears weird shirts. Or maybe they're not weird. They're more . . . interesting. And she saves me a seat. Or maybe the one next to her is never taken. I don't ask.

Tonight Beth is wearing a shirt that says NEVER TRUST AN ATOM. THEY MAKE UP EVERYTHING, and she is focused on the paper in her lap, which she's been folding for the past thirty minutes. Her dark-brown hair hangs over her face.

"Don't stop. That sounded *awesome*," Pastor Rick says with a beaming grin.

Even Ms. Sylvia, the choir director, blushes.

Pastor Rick leans against the piano. He's wearing a Pearl Jam shirt and tight dark jeans.

"You know, I sing a little myself," Pastor Rick says.

"Really?" Ms. Sylvia says.

"I even auditioned for *American Idol*."

"Did you make it?" a young girl in the room asks.

Pastor Rick shakes his head. "I realized I didn't need to perform for America's votes. I needed to impress the Big Guy instead." He looks at the ceiling.

I think I hear a girl behind me moan. Pastor Rick taps on the piano like he's thinking hard. "You wouldn't mind if I steal some of these fine young people for a bit? I need help setting up for the Harvest Festival this Sunday."

Almost everyone's hand shoots up—everyone but Beth and me.

"Eager volunteers," Pastor Rick says. *"Awesome."*

Beth mumbles beside me. "One . . . two . . . three . . . four . . . five . . ." She folds as she counts, then gets flustered and undoes the paper.

Pastor Rick asks Ms. Sylvia, "Do you ever listen to Pearl Jam?" Ms. Sylvia shakes her head. "Saw them at Lollapalooza a few years ago. Maybe we need to do a little grunge rock around here." Ms. Sylvia's eyes grow wide, and Pastor Rick touches her arm. "Just something to think about."

"Did he just say 'Lollapalooza'?" Beth whispers. "Loser."

"What?" I ask.

She looks up at me, surprised. "Are you talking to me?"

"Never mind," I say and turn away.

"No. No." Beth inches closer. "It's just, you don't say much."

And then I don't say much to that.

"Consistency. I like it." Beth laughs.

I look down at the paper in her hand. "What are you doing with that?"

"My science teacher said that if you fold a large piece of paper fifty times, the thickness would equal the distance from here to the sun. That's crazy, right?"

"You're trying to fold that paper fifty times?"

"The most I can get is five." Beth shakes her head, obviously a little frustrated. "Why are you in choir if you can't sing?"

"How do you know I can't sing?"

"I sit next to you."

A little laugh comes out of me. "I need to make friends."

"I'll be your friend." Beth shrugs. "I already know you can't sing. You're clearly not as impressed with Rick Wonder as everyone else is, so that's a good sign. And you like math."

"How do you know I like math?"

Beth points to my choir folder. It's covered in equations. I didn't realize how many I had written until now. I hug the folder to my chest, contemplating Beth's offer. But then she does this thing—she pulls a necklace from under her shirt. A cross necklace. She holds on to it like it's a life preserver, running the charm back and forth on the chain. It's hypnotizing. And speaks volumes.

Beth may not like Pastor Rick, but it's clear she loves Jesus. And people who love Jesus make me nervous, especially people who go to this church. I make the decision, right here, right now, that Beth and I cannot be friends. That is the truth. And we moved here to avoid consequences.

"Here's a math question for you," Beth says. "Is point nine recurring also equal to the number one?"

"That's easy," I say. "No."

"Is it?" Beth cocks an eyebrow at me. "Think about it, *friend*."

What I really need to think about is a way to break the truth to her.

∞

Hannah and I walk out of church as the sun sets, streaking the sky with purple, pink, and orange.

Here are a few notable things about the desert. Your lips will always be chapped. Your hair will always be staticky. Your skin will always be dry. You will get multiple nosebleeds. Mom will make you drink three full water bottles a day. Cacti and scorpions are the only things that thrive. And it never rains. Ever.

We walk across the lawn, past the gigantic Touchdown Jesus.

"Doesn't he scare you?" I ask Hannah. It's like asking a question to the wind. I watch my words get carried off into oblivion.

Hannah holds her Bible in her right hand.

Here are a few notable things about Hannah. She's an exact replica of Mom. Auburn hair. Blue eyes. Cantaloupe-sized breasts. When Mom goes to the grocery store, Hannah watches soap operas, because she likes all the kissing. She hates watermelon because of the texture. She writes "theatre" instead of "theater." She didn't carry around a Bible until about a year ago.

One more thing—she *was* my best friend.

"Why would I be scared of Jesus?" Hannah says. "He's all about love."

She walks away from me.

"When are you going to forgive me?" I ask. The words spill on the ground. The wind doesn't even bother picking them up.

Hannah glances over her shoulder and doesn't miss a step. She never misses a step. "It's not *my* forgiveness you need."

"But I'm sorry."

Here are a few notable things about Esther. I cry every time I watch *The Sound of Music*. I have short brown hair and brown eyes, which means I'm practically monochromatic. The texture of mango makes my teeth hurt. I look just like my deadbeat, nonexistent dad who left us so many years ago that I shouldn't be able to remember him. But I do. And most days, I'm not really sure there is a God. Or a Jesus.

Also, it's really hard to look like someone you hate but can't forget.

"Did you make any friends?" Mom asks as we drive away from church.

"A few," Hannah says. She turns up the radio and sings.

"What about you, Esther?" Mom asks over the music, keeping her eyes on the road.

"Not yet," I say.

"It'll happen."

I glance back at Jesus, at his hands outstretched to the sky, and wonder whether I could climb up and sit in his palm.

Maybe someday. When gravity doesn't exist, and the lone medium-sized dress in my closet actually fits.

∞

I stand over the toilet in our bathroom. It's super clean in here and smells like lemon.

I flush the toilet. The water swirls around and then disappears. It refills.

I dangle the picture of Amit and me over the toilet. It was taken at our eighth-grade graduation, when we both received the coveted "Pythagoras Award" for ranking first in math class. It was coveted to us, at least. Ms. Rainier insisted that Amit and I stand next to each other as she snapped a picture on her cell phone. Right before the flash went off, Amit put his arm around me.

Here's another notable thing about Esther—I was in love with Amit Kahn. He has really dark brown hair, just like me, but instead of brown eyes, his are a beautiful gold. And he made me laugh.

"You're really good at polynomials," he said once.

Amit is the reason we left the trampoline. Amit is the reason Hannah hates me. Amit is the reason we live in New Mexico. Knowing all of these facts, I can't seem to forget the time he told me that I was the coefficient to his variable. A girl just doesn't erase these magical moments from her mind. Which makes letting him go feel nearly impossible. But I need to.

Today, I will do it. Today, I will flush Amit down the toilet. At least the toilet is clean.

I look at the picture one more time, at Amit's fingers resting on my arm, at the closeness of his body to mine, and ask out loud, "How is it possible to feel a picture? You're one-dimensional."

> Complex Math Problem: Amit lives 1,300 miles away.
> He's banned from Esther's life forever. How can it still
> feel like he's holding her?

I think I might throw up. When that doesn't happen, instead of dropping the picture in the toilet, I promise myself I'll make some friends, just like Mom said. More than one. Then I brush my teeth and spit into the sink and don't wash it down.

The bathroom was clean. I messed it up. It seems to be a trend with me.

4

Truth or Consequences is a small town. It has one of everything—a pet store, a Chinese restaurant, a steak restaurant that advertises a daily $9.99 prime rib special, a coffee hut, a strip joint called Twin Peaks, an empty Blockbuster—to name a few things. It's so tiny people ride bikes everywhere.

Truth or Consequences is also situated right along the Rio Grande that, unlike our pool, is filled with water. The river is the only hydrated aspect of this town. A path runs along the Rio Grande. Mom insists that I need to ride my bike up and down it at least five times a day. That way, I'll fit into the summer dress by Christmas.

Most days, I take a nap in this old fallen tree that looks like a hammock. Tall bushes just off the trail cover it, so no one can see me.

And the sleep is good. The weird thing about living in a house that's full of nothing is that you're always waiting for something to come back. For something to walk in the door and take up space. Which makes sleeping tough. Things like to come back at night, when it's dark.

I nap along the river and oversleep today, jolting awake, surprised at where I am. This isn't anything new. Most days, I wake up here and for a second, I forget it all. That one second is the best moment of my day. Then it all comes back as a Niagara Falls–sized cascade of memories, and I think I'll drown. But there isn't enough water in Truth or Consequences to begin with, and it would be super selfish of me to take more than my share. Tom restricts us to five-minute showers already.

I splash water on my hair and shirt to make it look like I've been sweating, and then I start toward home. That's when I almost collide with a runner on the path.

"I'm sorry!" I yell over my shoulder, pedaling faster and catching a glimpse of his buzzed hair. "I didn't see you coming!"

He hollers back, "No one ever does!"

∞

Tom "volunteered" Hannah and me to run the "Fishers of Man" booth at the Touchdown Church's Harvest Festival. Kids walk from booth to booth in the church parking lot, collecting candy, prizes, and the Good News from God.

One side of the booth has a line of fish held captive in plastic bags. In the center are fishbowls. For three tickets, each kid can cast a line five times and try to make it into a bowl. Anyone who does gets a goldfish.

It's my job to hand over the fish and say, "And he saith unto them, Follow me, and I will make you fishers of men."

Tom said it was so easy I couldn't screw it up.

In the rest of the United States, today is Halloween. In Ohio, it's usually raining and cold, but that doesn't stop everyone from trick-or-treating. The air smells like wet leaves and pumpkin spice, and our neighbor does a graveyard display in his front yard and hides in a coffin, waiting to scare the crap out of the children. And the woman on the other side of our house gives out full-sized Snickers bars.

"Do you think they give out the big candy bars at this thing?" I ask Hannah as she lines up all the fishbowls perfectly.

"You shouldn't be thinking about that, Esther."

"Yeah, but do they?"

Hannah shakes her head, but I know she's thinking about the Snickers as much as I am.

"It doesn't matter," she says. "We're too old for trick-or-treating, and they'd just melt here anyway."

I cover my eyes and look up at the blue sky. The sun blazes down on the pavement, making it radiate. There's heat above us and below us. I am living in a kiln.

Hannah's right. It's like fall doesn't even exist here.

> Complex Math Problem: Two sisters are stuck in the desert of New Mexico. They're 1,300 miles from home. How many more miles will they have to travel before they smell rain again?

I squat down next to the table with the captive fish. They swim slowly from side to side in their temporary homes. Locking eyes with one, I get the feeling that I know this fish. It doesn't want to be here either.

"We have a winner," Hannah announces.

I take the captive fish and hand it over to Peter Marshfield, a boy from choir who's dressed in a tunic and holding a slingshot. He's a sophomore, and Hannah clearly likes the attention from an older guy.

"What's with the costume?" I ask.

Peter looks at me like I'm an idiot. "I'm David."

"Ignore her," Hannah says, so easily it hurts right in the center of my chest.

Peter looks at Hannah. "You're clearly dressed as an angel today."

I want to vomit.

Hannah encourages the flirting. "Keep the slingshot. I might need someone to slay a giant and save me one of these days."

Peter bulks out his muscleless, hairless chest. "See you at choir practice?"

"I'll save you a seat."

As Peter walks away, I holler after him, "And he saith unto them, Follow me, and I will make you fishers of men." Just like I'm supposed to say to all the winners, even if they seem like losers.

I lean back against the table and wipe sweat from my forehead. Tom says the air in the desert is dry, so people don't sweat. That's how he's able to wear long sleeves every day. I say the air in the desert is vampire air. It sucks the life out of you. Tom sometimes lies to make us feel better. I can't really fault him for it. Today is Halloween after all. People love to play pretend.

$$\infty$$

Five fish remain, each held captive in a plastic BPA-ridden bag. How did these fish find their way to the desert?

I can't answer that. It's too close to home.

"I'm sorry, little fish," I say, kneeling next to the table. "We're more alike than you think."

"Isn't it depressing?"

I stand up quickly, my legs numb from squatting.

The girl in front of me holds out her slushie. "Need a sip? It's hot out." My mouth is so dry I could sand a table. She shakes the slushie and smiles. "Come on, take it. You look like you need it."

At the exact same time, we recognize each other.

"The world's largest vacuum!" I say.

She points at me. "You're the funny girl!"

I laugh awkwardly and glance at Hannah, hoping she didn't hear that. Then a stroke of fear hits me as two worlds collide.

"You don't go to church here, do you?" I ask at once.

"I'm just here for the slushies," she says. "By the way, thanks for saving my ass with your sister. That was a close one."

"She's dramatic. I think she's just having a hard time adjusting."

"Right. Because you just moved here." And then she holds her arms out wide like she's hugging the world. "Welcome."

"Just to clarify . . ." I ask again. "You don't go to church here?"

"God, no. This festival is just better than sitting around thinking about how depressing Halloween is now. It's like I can see my innocence walking away in the Jedi costume I wore in fifth grade." She holds up her hand for me to high-five. "I'm Color, by the way. Shaking hands is too adult. I'm not *there* yet. Go on, give it a whack."

So I do. Our hands snap midair, sending tingles down my arm.

"Aggressive," Color says, shaking out her hand.

"Sorry. I haven't done that in a while."

"No, I like it. What's your name, Funny Girl?"

"Esther," I say, and kind of hope that my hand never stops tingling. For the first time since I started shriveling up in the desert, I feel alive. Eat it, cactus. "Color. That's an interesting name."

"I know. It's kind of weird. But my mom said that the world needs more color, and so she gave the world *me*, which is actually kind of beautiful." Color takes another sip. "That's my mom for you. Weird at times. Beautiful at times."

I can't tell by the way she says it whether that's a good thing or not.

"Seriously, you need a sip of this slushie . . ." Color hands it to me. When I take a gulp, it's like I'm transformed. Cherry Coke–flavored awesomeness. Color reads my mind. "I know, right?"

I hand it back a bit reluctantly. If I hold her drink hostage, maybe she won't leave. I *need* to keep talking to her.

"Do you want to play the game?" I ask.

Color shrugs. "No tickets." She squats down next to the goldfish. "They always give out fish at these things, knowing full well they'll be flushed down the toilet within a few weeks. It's like we're saying their lives are expendable, purely so kids can win something. It's so sad." She takes a pull from her straw. "Don't you think it's sad?"

Well, when you put it that way, it's totally sad, I think.

"I like your short hair, by the way," Color says. "I meant to tell you that the other day."

I touch my head instinctively. "Thanks."

"Short hair is so radical. It's like you're fighting the man by looking like a man, but clearly you're a woman." She points at my chest. "It's trippy."

She takes another pull of her slushie. Or maybe it's more like a drag. Or a hit.

"Oh my God!" She grabs the bridge of her nose. "Brain freeze! It hurts so bad!" She shakes her head clear. "Isn't it weird that we know some things will hurt us, but we do them anyway?"

I nod again. I've been transformed into a bobblehead.

Color looks at me with her intense gray eyes. I'm mesmerized by the shade. In a place that never sees rain, Color's eyes are the hue of storm clouds. "You know, I wasn't going to come to this thing today because that big Jesus statue kind of scares me, but then I thought, 'Don't let your fear prevent you from hitting up a radical festival with slushies.' And it turns out you're here. That's like a sign or something."

"It is?"

"Definitely," Color states without faltering. "But seriously, death by swirly." She points at the fish. "Can you imagine? I wish I had some tickets so I could save one." She takes another drag of her slushie and then shakes the cup. "Empty. So sad."

"Want to hear another joke?"

"Yes," Color says ardently.

"How does a fisherman determine how many fish he needs to catch to make a profit?"

"How?"

"By using a cod-ratic inequality."

She laughs, and it echoes across the parking lot, and suddenly everywhere around me is full of Color. "I don't get it at all! Which only makes it even funnier!"

I want to ask her a million questions. Why does she clean houses when she looks like she's my age? How does she really feel about her mom? What's her favorite slushie flavor? Who does she get her eyes from—Mom or Dad? Will she be my friend?

"I better go," Color says, sounding disappointed. "But hey, I'll see you on Tuesday."

"You will?"

"Yeah, when I come to clean your house."

And I swear, at this moment, the sky gets brighter and I don't mind living in a kiln so much.

"Great," I say.

"Great," Color says.

Great. Mom can't get mad at me. Even she said I need to make friends.

∞

One fish remains. I can't leave it. Death by swirly. It's too awful. I go to the ticket booth and pay five dollars for twenty tickets.

"What are you doing?" Hannah asks when I return.

I hand her three tickets. "I want to play."

"Why?"

"Because."

"Just answer the question, Esther."

"I thought you were the one with all the answers, *Hannah.*"

She hands me a fishing pole, grudgingly. "You are so annoying."

It takes eighteen tickets for me to win. When I do, I jump up and down. It's like I'm back on our old trampoline, cool Ohio air breezing through my hair. Hannah hands over the last fish.

"You have to say it."

Hannah groans. "And he saith unto them, Follow me, and I will make you fishers of men."

5

The one pet store in Truth or Consequences is in the one strip mall, next to the one Chinese restaurant, which is next to the one empty Blockbuster.

I buy a fishbowl, a bag of colorful stones, and a canister of fish food. Tom said that if I want to have a fish, I have to take care of it myself, which means paying for it. Then Mom slipped me twenty dollars and said, "Tom is ridiculous sometimes."

The store is loud with chirping.

"Have you ever been to California?" I ask the cashier.

"No."

"Me neither."

"It's pretty far from here."

I put everything in my backpack.

"It's a thousand miles," I say.

"You planning to go there or something?" He points at my baby-blue cruiser bike parked in front of the store. It only has three speeds. "Might take a while." He has a goatee, gray hair, and a red apron covered in cat hair.

"No. But I've already come thirteen hundred miles. What's one thousand more?"

"If you say so." He looks at me with a confused expression. "Shouldn't you be in school?"

I shake my head. "There are cracks at public school. It's too easy to fall."

"What does that mean?"

It's just so loud in here. I cover my ears. "Where is all that noise coming from?"

"My canaries. You want to see 'em?"

"No, thank you." I leave the pet store immediately. But even outside, the chirping is still in my head.

> Complex Math Problem: Esther is aware that California exists. Tom thinks California is in the past. Mom knows better. But canaries caught in a cage can't fly west. How long will it take for Esther to free herself?

∞

I decide to try coffee. I'm just so damn tired. I ride my bike to the one coffee hut in town, a place called HuggaMug Café. It's meant for cars, but I ride up to the window and say, with emphasis, "Beep!"

A boy with light-brown hair, perfectly waved over his forehead, opens the window and looks down at me.

"Well, this is a first."

"I'd like a coffee," I say.

"Just a coffee."

"Yes."

"You look more interesting than just a coffee," he says.

"I do?"

"I'm kind of a matchmaker when it comes to this stuff."

"You are?"

He nods. "You look like an iced soy mocha frap to me."

"I do?"

"Do you trust me?"

"That's kind of a loaded question."

"I'm kind of a loaded person."

"Well," I say. "Since I've never had coffee before, I guess I have to trust you."

"You've never had coffee before?!" He leans out the window. "How do you *survive?*"

He asks earnestly, so I answer the same way. "Barely. I barely survive."

"Oh, *mon chéri*, let me bring you back to life. Wait here." He closes the window.

I put the kickstand down and wait. A few minutes later, he reappears in the window, holding a large drink.

"Time to start living again," he says and hands it to me. I take a sip, and it's the most delicious thing I have ever tasted. He grins widely, exposing a perfect set of white teeth. "Am I good or what?"

"You're good." I take another sip, then I catch his name tag and spit some of my delicious drink out. "Your name is Jesus?" I yell, a little too loudly.

He groans. "The accent is so faded, you can't see it." And then the boy who brought me back to life leans out the window and kisses me on the cheek. "It's actually pronounced Hey-soos. My name is Jesús."

∞

"You saved a fish!" Color drops the vacuum and runs over to my windowsill. "You did it, Esther!"

"I don't know if I saved it so much as I put it in another container."

Color waves off my comment. "The whole world is one big container. Everyone's a hostage. That's life."

When she puts it that way, I don't feel so alone.

"What did you name it?" she asks.

"I didn't think about that."

"Names are important, Esther. My brother's name is Moss, and he's a total fungus." She plops down on my bed.

"You have a brother?"

Color nods, and I can tell by the gentle expression on her face that she really does love him, so I don't bother telling her that moss is actually a plant, not a fungus. She lies back on my bed with a harrumph and pats for me to lie next to her. And then we just stay there for a while, staring at the ceiling.

"You need some glow-in-the-dark stars," she says. She rolls to her side and props her head in her hand. "So you finally cleaned your room."

I hope she keeps talking. I like that Color says things that are unpredictable, which makes me feel more awake, like I'm actually living, not just surviving.

"OK," Color says, "I have to tell you the truth."

"Are you sure you want to do that? You don't really know me."

"You saved a fish, Esther. That says something."

And I believe her. "Go for it."

"Your sister wasn't completely wrong about me," she says. "I kind of steal stuff from people's trash. I'm a klepto-dumpster-diving-maniac. But it doesn't feel like stealing, because people are getting rid of the stuff in the first place. It's more like I'm *saving* things from being lost in a landfill, forever. Doesn't that sound horrible? Lost in old Band-Aids and Styrofoam cups that never decompose. I figure it's part of my job as a cleaner. But I only take from people I know."

The vacuum is still running.

"I just needed you to know. And now that I've said it out loud, I feel better." Color grins. "OK, what about you? Tell me something about Esther."

For a second, I'm thrown. People usually tell *me* about me—Mom, Tom, even Hannah. They tell *me* what to do, when to do it, how to do it.

I get off the bed and open my closet, exposing stacks of unpacked boxes. And then I lift my bed skirt, and Color sees the full extent of what I'm hiding.

"I didn't really clean my room. I just hid everything."

She laughs, jovially and loudly, with her entire body, and I swear the sound fills the hole in my chest where the wind blows through at night and echoes, lonely.

"Well, if you ever want to get rid of anything, I'm happy to take on the burden," Color says when her giggles have calmed. And with a glance at the clock in my room, which reads 2:30 p.m., she stands up quickly. "Crap. I better get back to work." She pauses. "Wait. Shouldn't you be in school or something?"

"Technically," I say. "I am in school."

"You're homeschooled!" Color is a ball of excitement again, and my room fills with her energy. "That's so awesome. What grade are you in?"

"I'm a sophomore."

"Me, too! So have you ever gone to a regular school?"

Words clog my throat. I nod, once.

"Which do you like better?" she asks.

"Regular school," I say, unwilling to say more but unable to hold back a wave of memories. The smell of dry-erase markers. Organizing a backpack for the first day. Holding a hand as I walk the halls between classes. I can practically feel Amit's fingers laced between mine.

Color places her hand on my arm. "They just teach us lies in high school anyway. You're not missing out."

"I'm pretty sure it's the same at my house," I say. "What about you? Shouldn't you be in school?"

Color goes back to the vacuum and moves it back and forth over a spot she had already covered. "I go half a day three days a week so I can work in the afternoons. The school calls it 'Skills for Living Co-Op.'" She shakes her head. "Let's just say with my mom, knowing how to clean up other people's garbage comes in handy."

I want to know more about Color and her high school and her family, but Mom knocks on the door and pokes her head in my room like a turtle.

"We need to leave in five minutes," she says. "And don't forget your water bottle."

"Got it."

She notices my clean room. "You finally put everything away. I knew it wouldn't take too long. It feels good, doesn't it?" But she closes the door before I can answer.

Color gives me a knowing smile, puts her earbuds back in, and continues vacuuming.

I pull a box of my old sports equipment from the closet—tennis racket, soccer ball, softball, and an old pair of adjustable roller skates, the kind that strap on to your shoes. I just want Color to have something. "Here." I hand her the roller skates.

"You opened a box for *me*?"

I guess I didn't think about it that way, or any way at all.

She hugs the skates to her chest. "I promise I'll take good care of these, Esther."

"I know." I smile. "You're saving them."

Color cringes. "Used Band-Aids. So gross."

∞

The magazines at the doctor's office are dated. I pick one up and thumb through old gossip. Then I put it back down. My hands feel dirty just from touching the sticky cover, and I rub them on my legs, which won't stop shaking, even though Mom has put her hand on my thigh at least one hundred times since we've been here.

"It's just a checkup," she says. "A . . . precaution."

That's a lie. This is a punishment. A way for her to remind me what a doctor's office smells like, how cold the tile is on your feet, how embarrassing it is to wear a gown that opens in back. How alone and unprepared you feel with your feet nestled in stirrups. Mom wants to make sure I never want to be here again. My doctor in Ohio said it was over, and this is Mom's way of clarifying the point here in New Mexico.

She doesn't tell me to relax or take a deep breath. With her hand on my thigh, Mom stills my shuddering body. Like gravity reminds you that the earth is always beneath your feet. The earth will always hold you, even when other people won't.

But it doesn't feel like that right now. It feels like I'm out of my body and floating, but it's not a serene hovering. It's more chaotic and unpredictable. At any moment, I might collapse.

I can't bring myself to look at Mom. Mom can't even bring herself to look at me. We both stare at the dirty stack of magazines and the green carpet that resembles fake grass. Every few minutes the phone rings, and the receptionist acts angry that it does.

"I spy with my little eye," Mom whispers, leaning into me. It's the game we always played in the pediatrician's office when Hannah and I were young. Mom would keep us occupied, looking around the room for colored objects, while we waited for the doctor or when we had to get a shot. "Something . . ." But this isn't the pediatrician's office, and Mom doesn't have time to finish.

"Esther Wyatt." The name echoes in my head. I slowly glance at the nurse. "Esther Wyatt."

Mom stands and slings her purse over her shoulder.

"Esther Ainsworth. My last name is Wyatt," Mom says. "I'm remarried."

Ainsworth is my dad's last name. I am made up of all things Dad. But he doesn't matter anymore. That's what Mom said twelve years ago when I asked her where Dad went. I was four.

"He doesn't matter anymore." Those were her exact words.

But I'm made up of all of his matter. I have his hair and his eyes and his skin.

Complex Math Problem: If Dad doesn't matter, and I'm made up of him, do I matter?

I finally look up from the carpet. "I want to go by myself."

Mom pauses, a frown pulling her cheeks downward.

"Please," I say.

And she concedes.

The nurse takes me away, and I glance at Mom before the door shuts. She still isn't looking at me. She wants to escape this as much as I do, but she holds on out of worry, and I hold on out of heartbreak.

The nurse records my weight and blood pressure and writes numbers on my chart.

The paper crinkles under my weight when I sit down on the exam table.

"Dr. Rodriguez will be in, in a moment," the nurse says.

My mind is distant, unable to concentrate as the nurse talks, the beige walls overtaking my vision. Now I know why Tom wanted to move to the desert. It's plain here. A landscape of neutral colors. And always sunny. He wants me to be plain and sunny.

"Do you have any questions?" the doctor asks as she enters.

"Questions?"

Dr. Rodriguez flips through my chart.

Do I have any *more* questions?

"What did the Little Mermaid wear?"

"Pardon?"

"An algae-bra."

Dr. Rodriguez sets my chart down. "Are you OK, Esther?"

"It's a joke. Get it?"

She looks at me as if I'm a pathetic puppy. "Any other questions?"

"Does it ever rain in the desert?" I ask.

"Not very often." Dr. Rodriguez tells me to take care of myself and to let her know if I need anything in the future.

But I'm not concerned about my future. It's my past that's following me.

∞

The pool is warm beneath my body, and while I know I'm lying still, one part of me can't stop running. Memories aren't easily forgotten or censored when you're sixteen. Some days, I'll just be lying here and the past will creep up behind me and tap me on the shoulder, like a kind librarian. It feels nice, comforting, and before I know it, I'm turning around to stare into golden eyes, wishing I could just ignore him, but knowing that's impossible. And in that moment, the past becomes the present again.

"Hey, Esther," he says.

"Yeah, Amit."

One side of his mouth pulls down more than the other, creating this beautifully crooked smile, and right at the crown of his head, a cowlick forces up a little tuft of hair no matter how often he attempts to flatten it. When Amit moves to smooth his hair, I stop him. I like that his hair sticks up. And even though I'm reaching for something that only exists in my memory, I swear I feel him. I feel the bump on the knuckle of his left ring finger from years of holding a pencil the wrong way. Where other boys have calluses from sports and weight lifting, Amit's palm is smooth, like silk. I press my thumb directly into its center. It fits perfectly, like I'm a piece of his puzzle.

"What did one algebra book say to the other?" Amit asks.

"What?"

"Don't bother me. I've got my own problems."

And I laugh and laugh and laugh, until tears stream down my cheeks, Amit dissolving in front of me, the puzzle falling apart into infinitesimal pieces, and I realize I'm sobbing.

6

Music with a heavy beat spills out of HuggaMug Café as I ride up. Through the glass I see Jesús bouncing and throwing napkins around the hut like they are confetti. He sees me and opens the window, out of breath.

"Mon chéri! Back for another iced soy mocha frap?"

"You remember?"

"I never forget a coffee. Wait. Are you crying?"

"No." I wipe tears from my face. "I have dust in my eyes."

But my face is swollen. I can feel it. Dust doesn't do that, but Jesús doesn't question me further. He just hands me a napkin.

"For the dust," he says.

"Can I have something to bring me back to life?" I say.

He nods and disappears. Then he returns, and the music is even louder. "Mon chéri, I love this song! We *need* to dance."

He climbs out the window and pulls me off my bike. The music is blaring. I don't know the song, but all of a sudden, I'm dancing in the middle of the street with the boy who brought me back to life, and all of my worries are gone. Jesús twirls me in a circle. I laugh and begin to get dizzy, and the more I laugh, and the dizzier I get, the lighter I feel.

When the song is over, I'm giggling so hard my stomach hurts, and I almost fall over. Jesús catches me in a hug and whispers, "Sometimes, you just need to dance to shake off the dust. And this is the desert. It can get really dusty."

Another boy hangs his head out the window. "What the hell are you doing? Get back in here and clean this shit up."

Jesús yells over his shoulder. "It's called *Hug*gaMug. I'm just doing my job." He kisses me on the cheek. "I hope I've been of service today. Please don't hesitate to fill out a comment card and remark on my fabulous dance skills. I'm also pretty talented with a frothing wand."

"Seriously, dude," the other boy says.

I grab Jesús's arm before he can walk away. "You have. Helped. Today."

"Then my job is done." He winks at me. "Come back and see us soon. I'm here every Tuesday, Thursday, and Saturday."

"I mean it. I'm not cleaning up your fucking mess, Jesús," the other boy says.

"I love it when you get all teenage angsty," Jesús replies. He looks back at me. "He needs to froth some milk, if you know what I mean."

Jesús goes back into the hut, through the side door, and reemerges at the window. "Don't be a stranger, mon chéri."

I climb back on my bike. "Why the French?"

Jesús says, "If this hut can pretend to be a *café*, I figure I can pretend to be French. It feels better than the reality most days."

"Then . . . au revoir."

"Adieu." Jesús blows me a kiss.

I ride away from the coffee hut without my iced soy mocha frap, but I got what I came for. I feel better.

And the other boy who yelled at Jesús—I think I've seen his buzzed head before.

∞

Rebekah Crane

It turns out .9 recurring is totally equal to 1. I'm still trying to wrap my head around this fact when I walk into choir practice on Wednesday. I worked on it all last night.

Obviously, ⅓ × 3 = 1.

And .3 recurring × 3 = .9 recurring.

Also, ⅓ and .3 recurring are the same number.

That means .9 recurring is equal to 1.

Beth looks in my direction and then at the empty seat next to her. I sit down in it.

"You figured it out, didn't you?" she says.

I nod. "Thank you."

"For what?"

I was so concentrated on figuring out the problem last night that I didn't have time to think about anything else. Not the cactus outside my window, or the picture of Amit tucked under my mattress, or how Hannah used to crawl into bed with me when she was cold in the winter. She'd put her freezing toes in between my hot legs, and it drove me crazy, but eventually we'd fall asleep, tangled together. All that has changed. We live *here* now.

I don't know how to answer Beth's question. Thank her *for what?* For taking me out of the past and giving me a problem I *can* solve. She might ask more questions.

And she's grabbing at her cross necklace again.

Ms. Sylvia starts practice with an announcement that next week she's holding solo auditions for our upcoming Christmas performance. Anyone interested should sign the clipboard she passes around the room. Hannah, who is sitting next to Peter, signs.

Ms. Sylvia says that we're going to learn the Smashing Pumpkins song "Christmastime" to spice things up a bit, on Pastor Rick's recommendation. Beth groans.

As we practice, I see Peter flirting with Hannah, who tosses her long hair like she's a horse. For the past week, she's been lying out by our

38

empty pool. Now she has a summer glow in November. She's a cactus in the desert.

But me . . . I wake up every morning hoping I'll smell rain, hoping I'll fill a backpack with school supplies and walk down our street in Ohio to the bus stop. The high school bus comes at six forty-five in the morning, and in the winter it's always late. Mr. Bob gets nervous driving in the snow. When I finally arrive at school, Amit stands at my locker. He takes my frozen hands, bringing them to his mouth, and blows his warm breath on the tips of my fingers. High school is noisy in the morning, but Amit and I seem to live in a bubble, untouched by the sounds of overly caffeinated teenagers.

The tips of my fingers press together, too warm for their own good in November. I turn to Beth and whisper desperately, "Do you have any more math problems for me?"

Beth thinks for a second, and I can tell by her face that she's got a lot going on. Today her shirt says: **OBEY GRAVITY. IT'S THE LAW**. Beth must be smart. Like really smart. And I like smart people, but that darn necklace makes me not want to like her. It makes it so I *can't* like her. She probably follows all the commandments, *all* the rules, and I don't. Or at least haven't . . . in the past.

"It's not really a question, more like a mind bender. Do you think you can handle it?" Beth asks.

I need a mind bender. Please, twist my brain in a new direction.

Beth gets excited. "OK. This is a fact. Most people have more than the average number of legs."

"Right," I say.

"But if *most* have more—then how is it the average?"

My head tries to wrap around what she's said. How can that be true?

"I know, right?" Beth says. "It's crazy."

Then Ms. Sylvia taps her wand on her music stand and clears her throat.

Beth leans in, still smiling, and says, "Do you want to hang out sometime?"

Everything inside my body sags lower, threatening to fall to the floor in a splat. I can practically hear it groan.

Beth grabs at her cross necklace. What if she finds out? Will she tell everyone at church?

Across the room, Hannah flirts with Peter, wiping hair from his forehead. She always has the answers. But when she looks back at me, her gaze is like daggers. Message received.

I agreed to the deal. Tom said if we made a fresh start, we'd all keep our mouths shut, and pretend like nothing ever happened. But when he said it, it felt more like a threat, like if one of our mouths opened, it would all come tumbling down.

I can't do that to Hannah again. She may not want to climb into bed with me anymore, but I'm the one who made us move. I put her bed in a different city where it's always sunny and warm.

I can't be friends with Beth.

Choir practice ends, and I never answer Beth's question. I feel bad about that. After all, I know how it feels. But I don't want to disappoint Beth by giving her an answer she won't like.

∞

Tonight I've decided to try singing Smashing Pumpkins with my head stuffed under my pillow. But after just a few minutes, I start to sweat and then to suffocate. Flopping onto my back, I stare up at the bare ceiling.

"Are you sure this is OK?" Amit asks. He's lying next to me. His body is the exact length of mine.

"No." I laugh. He would come over when Mom went to her Wednesday afternoon Zumba class and Hannah had ballet lessons. Tom came home from work promptly at six thirty, which meant Amit and I had two hours in the house to ourselves. Freedom at our fingertips. I'd take him up to my room, and Amit would look around, aghast to be in a girl's room, skittish, rubbing the back of his neck.

"Don't worry. No one will be home for a while. I just want to show you something."

I feel Amit turn his head in my direction, as if he's lying next to me in New Mexico, and not locked in a memory of Ohio. "What do you want to show me, Esther?"

My hand touches the empty side of my bed. "Let's start with everything."

∞

"What's your favorite thing you've saved from the landfill?" I ask. Color and I are lying at the bottom of the empty pool on Tuesday. It's been a week since I saw her last. She glances at me but doesn't answer the question. She just smiles, like she has a secret, the best kind of secret.

"What do you do out here, anyway?" she asks.

"Nothing, really. I just lie here." I look at her to see what she thinks, and Color gazes serenely up at the sky. I swear it smiles back. "It's better than being inside all the time."

"I get it," Color says. "My mom isn't big on walls either. They hold too many things in."

"And she doesn't like to hold things in?"

"No. She doesn't want to be contained." Color looks at me. "There's a difference."

One lonely white cloud hangs above us.

Mom and Hannah are at the grocery store. I asked to stay home, and Mom said that was a good idea, to make sure the cleaning company doesn't try to steal anything else. I had to control my laughter.

"Can I tell you the truth, though?" Color says, rolling onto to her side.

41

"Sure."

"Sometimes I wish my mom would be contained just a little bit. Like just to the state of New Mexico."

"She doesn't live here?"

Color shakes her head. "Not right now. She kind of comes and goes. She's taking care of my grandma in Denver at the moment. I know, sounds like a really nice thing to do, right? But really she's just scamming on my granny's money because Granny's too old to know any better."

"You live with your dad, then?"

"God, no. He lives somewhere in Scotland. My mom promises I'll meet him one day, but I don't know. She's not so good with promises, so we'll see."

"Who do you live with, then?"

"It's just me and Moss." Color points up. "That cloud looks like one of those half-horse, half-people things."

I feel myself staring at Color too long. She lives alone with her brother. And no dad, just like me. "A centaur," I say.

"Yes! A centaur." Color is bright in the sunshine today, even when she talks about sad things, like missing parents and scamming money off old people. "So did you think of a name for your fish yet?"

"Not yet."

"It'll come to you, Esther."

We lie there for a long time without saying anything. It's comfortable. The centaur gallops away. I don't want to move from this spot. I *know* what it feels like to be abandoned, to feel like no matter how hard you hold on to something, it all turns to sand in your grasp. And if Color is lonesome, I want to just lie here and make her feel full. Make her feel whole. I grab her hand. She flinches, but then she interlaces her fingers with mine.

When Mom knocks on the sliding glass door, it surprises us both. We sit up.

Mom sticks her head outside and looks at us suspiciously. "Esther, help me unload the groceries."

I dust the paint chips off my butt. The pool needs to be resealed if it's ever to hold water again. Color laughs and wipes more flecks from my back, the part I can't reach or see, and I do the same for her.

"So we should hang out sometime," Color says as she climbs the ladder. I think I might burst. I wait for Tuesday all week. It's the only day when living in the desert doesn't make me feel shriveled up.

> Complex Math Problem: When one broken piece joins together with another broken piece, is it considered whole again, even if the edges don't match up perfectly?

Mom watches me through the sliding glass door.

"I'd love to hang out," I say.

Color gets excited. "This Friday. You know where the Blockbuster is?"

It's a small town. I already know where everything is. "Yes."

"Meet us there," Color says. "Seven o'clock."

Color and I walk through the open sliding door. She says to Mom, "You have a really nice house."

Mom says, "Thank you."

"And I totally get why you don't fill the pool," Color adds. "Safety first."

Mom turns to me with one of those looks that speaks. It says, *Listen up, Esther.* "That's right," she says to Color. "Safety first."

It's not until Color leaves that I realize she said to meet *us*.

7

My eyes catch the boy with the buzzed hair running down by the river and I chase after him. I don't know why. Maybe it's because he works with Jesús. Maybe it's because I've seen him running before. Maybe it's because this is a small town, and I barely know anyone, and for some reason I feel like I know him. He looks so familiar. I jump on my bike and ride up next to him.

He glances back at me. "What are you doing?"

"I saw you the other day," I say. "At HuggaMug."

"So?"

Good question. So what?

"Don't be mad at Jesús. He was just trying to cheer me up."

The boy with the buzz haircut is running really fast, and I have to pedal hard to keep up with him.

"Jesús knows I can't stay mad at him."

The boy's legs move so swiftly I barely believe someone can run at this speed. He's practically floating just above the ground. And he's not even winded.

"I see you running a lot," I say out of breath.

"So?"

At least he's consistent.

"What are you running from?"

He stops abruptly and puts his hands on his hips, his breathing more labored now. I skid my bike to a halt.

"Who said I'm running from anything?" he asks.

Good question. Why did I put it that way?

"Isn't everyone running from something?"

He looks me up and down with intense gray eyes. He's wearing one of those wicking shirts that clings tight to his chest. He's thin but muscular.

How do I know him?

I feel sweat drip down my back and also collect around my ears. Inadvertently, this boy has gotten me to work out, just what Mom wants me to do.

"Never mind," I say and get back on my bike.

I'm about to ride away when he says, "I run cross-country."

I stop, hesitantly glancing at him.

"I've seen you sleeping here before. Why do you sleep?"

He asks the question honestly, so I answer the same way.

"To escape," I say.

His eyes travel down to his shoes. "It's the same with running."

He starts down the trail again, running even faster than before, almost rejuvenated. That or he really doesn't want to talk to me. I don't follow him, because it's hard to escape when someone's riding your tail and you have to look back constantly when you should keep your eyes forward.

But the boy with the buzzed hair asks really good questions. I may have met my match.

∞

I ask Mom if I can go out tonight. It's Friday. We're standing in the kitchen making dinner. Tom is still at the bank. Mom fills up my "Esther" water bottle and sets it down next to me.

"With who?"

I keep my head down as I chop onions for the spaghetti sauce. They sting my eyes.

"Color. The girl who cleans our house," I say. "You said we need to make friends."

"Color," Mom says. "Interesting name." She doesn't answer my question right away, but takes some of the chopped onions and adds them to the cooking meat. I keep dicing as tears begin to form in my eyes and fall down my cheeks.

"You know, I wanted to name you Violet, but your dad didn't like names that were colors, like Ruby and Hazel." Mom tucks loose auburn hair behind her ear. Hannah does the same motion with her hair, too.

"Amber . . . Jade . . . Goldie?" I say.

"How about Olive?"

"Raven?"

"Scarlet."

I gag.

"I still love the name Violet, though," Mom says. "It's nice for a girl."

"I like it, too." I keep chopping. Mom keeps cooking. I add more onions to the pot. She turns to me then, with tears running down her face, just like mine. We stare at each other. It's the wettest thing to happen in the desert since we arrived.

I ask Mom in my head, *Why did you let this happen?* It's the most selfish thing I've ever asked because I *made* this happen. I wrote the equation and asked Mom and Tom to answer it. And they did.

"From the onions," Mom says, with a sniffle that knows it's a lie. I hand her a napkin. She points at the "Esther" water bottle as she pats her face dry. "Drink that." I follow her orders. Mom says, "Color. I like that name." Then she adds, "Just let me deal with Tom."

∞

Mom is a liar, which I knew, but somehow managed to forget in the move. She tells Tom that I'm going out with Beth from church. She says it so smoothly, I almost believe her.

Hannah sits in her seat, frowning.

I ignore her. It's what she wants anyway. Tom says that as long as I'm home by ten, he doesn't see a problem with it. A napkin is tucked into the collar of his long-sleeved button-down shirt, so he doesn't slurp spaghetti sauce on it, but he doesn't roll up his sleeves. I see the tail of his snake tattoo. I swear it rattles at me.

When Mom drives me to the Blockbuster in her old, run-down van, I ask her why she lied.

"Esther, why do you think I drive this piece of shit?" The question throws me, not only because it's not an answer, but also because when Mom swears, it's like she becomes herself again. Right there in the front seat—she's transformed into the woman who worked as a grocery store manager for eight years. Who brought home life-sized cardboard cutouts of famous people from displays at the store, just so we could have Brad Pitt at our dinner table. The woman who likes multicolored Christmas lights instead of the white ones Tom makes us put up.

"Why?" I ask.

Mom pulls into the strip mall's lot and parks. "Because every woman should have something of her own. Her *very* own." Mom gestures to the Blockbuster. "I'm letting you have this, Esther. No funny business this time. Don't let my lie go to waste."

I swallow the sudden lump in my throat.

"I'll pick you up at ten," she says. Then she pulls her ponytail free, letting long auburn hair cascade down her back, and turns up the radio. I hear her sing at the top of her lungs as she pulls out of the parking lot.

At the door of the Blockbuster, I pause, the reason for meeting here unknown. But I invited her to lie in an empty pool. Who am I to judge? Paper covers the windows, so I can't see inside. The place feels totally abandoned.

The doors open within a few seconds, and Color pops her head out.

"You're here!" she shouts, and grabs my arm to yank me inside. And as the doors close, Color says, "Esther, welcome to Heaven."

8

Heaven is an old, boarded-up Blockbuster. It's filled with all sorts of items—a tricycle, a pogo stick, a few rocking chairs, rugs, an old TV and VCR, books, paintings. There's even an entire wall of random family photos. The space is large and echoes, and yet it doesn't feel cavernous. The lights are dim, casting a soft glow on everything. The luminescence fills the room and practically radiates warmth.

I notice two accessories I *really* wasn't expecting to find.

"Iced soy mocha frap?" Jesús says. "Is that you?"

"What is *she* doing here?" the boy with the buzzed hair says at the same time.

Color says, "You guys know each other?"

Jesús answers by running up and grabbing me in a hug. "Mon chéri, this is unexpected. I love when things like this happen. It's kismet."

"Oh my God, this is so meant to be! I didn't know you knew each other!" Color gestures animatedly. "Isn't this amazing? You just went from being in the universe to being in *our* universe. It's like BAM! Life-changing moment right now. The universe totally wanted all of us to be friends!"

"Stop speaking for the universe," the boy with the buzzed hair says.

I'm speechless. How are they all here? How did this happen? And is this really Heaven? It feels that way. I feel euphoric.

"I can't believe *this* is the girl you were talking about," the boy with the buzzed hair says to Color, and I finally know where I've seen him before. I've seen *her* in him. He looks exactly like Color.

"Fungus," I say as it all clicks in my head.

Jesús puts his arm around me. "You're already fitting in."

"It's Moss," he says harshly. "*Moss.* And how do we know if we can trust you?"

"Fungus, you need to get laid," Jesús says. "Then maybe you wouldn't be so grouchy. I bet a good old-fashioned hand job would even do the trick. You don't need a girlfriend for one of those." Jesús winks at me.

"You would know," Moss snaps.

"You can trust Esther," Color says. "She saved my ass. And a fish."

I walk around the room, still in shock, checking out all of the accessories. Color follows me, riding on the tricycle, her knees up in her chest. I find the pair of roller skates I gave her.

"Is all of this the stuff you've taken?" I ask. "But how—"

"Our mom owns the space," Color answers before I can finish the question. It's like she's in my brain, like the universe wants us together. "She had a Blockbuster franchise until she realized that movie rentals were contributing to childhood obesity, and the universe didn't like that, so she gave up on the business."

"Also, Netflix was invented," Moss adds from across the room.

"That, too." Color shrugs. "She gave us the space as a gift. To do whatever we want with it. So we created Heaven. It's better than the landfill."

"And it was a secret until now," Moss says.

"Secrets, secrets are no fun. Secrets, secrets hurt someone," Jesús chides.

"Not in my book," Moss scoffs.

"Why do you call it 'Heaven'?" I ask.

"Well, it's kind of like all of these things died. I saved them and brought them here—to the afterlife. Plus, what's the safest place in the universe? *Heaven.*" Color literally sounds like heaven when she says that.

I stand in front of the wall with the framed family pictures.

"People throw these out?" I ask.

Jesús comes up next to me on the pogo stick. "I wish I could throw my family out." He bounces up and down, eyes on the pictures. Then a wide grin grows on his face. "You haven't even seen the best part."

"Don't," Moss says firmly.

"Stop being a fungus, Fungus."

Moss groans from across the room like Jesús is an asshole. He's sitting in an old oversized armchair, eating from a bag of potato chips.

"We should show her," Color says to Jesús. His eyes sparkle with excitement, and he bounces enthusiastically across the room, like a gigantic bunny.

"I warned you!" Moss calls after us.

Color leads me to the back of the store and stops in front of an archway that has no door, just a red velvet curtain hanging over the entrance. Above the curtain are the words "Adults Only."

"This is the old porn section," she says. "Many a lonely soul wandered behind this curtain, looking for comfort."

"Comfort? Is that what we're calling it now?" Jesús smiles. "God, I love to comfort myself."

"Multiple times a day," Moss says, walking up behind us. I peek over my shoulder at him, startled. Our eyes connect. He has the same gray eyes as Color. Moss bites down on a chip and says with his mouth full, "In your case, that is, Jesús."

"It's important for the soul." Jesús pats his heart, and then his hand moves down to his pants. "And my frothing wand."

"The symbolism is kind of perfect," Color says. "The world is filled with desperate people seeking solace and acceptance, but it isn't until they pass behind a protective curtain that they can finally admit who they are. And they can be free."

"Amen," Jesús says. "I speak for every gay kid hiding behind the world's heaviest closet door. Or curtain in this instance."

With a momentary glance at Jesús, I ask in my head, *Are you gay?* Jesús winks at me then.

"Color, only you would be able to make a bunch of lonely men with boners sound eloquent." Moss shakes his head.

Color dusts her shoulder off and then wraps her arm around me. She covers me in this open space where things thought dead come back alive. I know how these items feel. This might really be heaven.

"Are you ready, Esther?" she asks.

Are you ready, Esther?

A memory pulls. The question echoes in my mind. It's attached to a string that threatens to pull me back to the past.

"Don't say I didn't warn you," Moss says.

Color yanks back the curtain.

What I see . . . is absolutely beautiful.

9

Every color of the rainbow fills my eyes. I ask the universe Color believes in, *Is this real?* I run my hand over the walls. It has to be real. Life is on the walls in front of me, splattered in words and pictures.

"Do you like it?" Color asks.

I nod slowly and Jesús squeals.

"How did . . . what . . ." I can't find my words.

"It was Color's brilliant idea," Jesús says. "She wanted a place for . . . everything."

"Not everything is an object you can steal," Color says. "But even our thoughts deserve a home. A place to . . . belong."

Moss sits on the ground with his knees pulled up to his chest. He looks like a little boy. The light illuminates his face, making his eyes sparkle and enveloping him in a radiant halo. Color carries the same glow. And so does Jesús. I wonder if here, right now in the porn section of Blockbuster, I have a halo, too.

I trace the words written on the walls. "Lust" is written in red marker. Next to the word is a list of names: Sam, Louis, Pedro, Joel, Brett.

I look at Jesús. He says, "If I can't have them, I had to hold them somewhere."

There are maps of Scotland, India, and the United States tacked to the wall. Without thinking, dazed by all that's around me, my hand reaches out to touch California, knowing this moment is the closest I've come to actually being there. My fingers trace a disjointed, illogical route all the way back to Ohio.

"It's just a place for us to put all the things that we feel don't have a place," Color says, breaking my trance. "Like all those lost, random thoughts that swirl around in your head. They go here." She touches the wall.

Words are everywhere. All connecting. It's everything that exists in the universe in one room captured on three walls and closed off by a curtain. I feel the words, each letter wrapped around me, encasing me, telling me I belong, too.

"This place really is heaven," I say.

With a bucket of markers in her hands, Color dances toward me, like she's tempting me with a tango.

"Now it's your turn, Esther," she says, twirling me in a circle. "Add something lost to the walls, so it can be found."

"But I don't know what to write." I take a step back, my head swirling slightly from Color's spin. I'm kind of lying, because I don't know if there was a single part of me that wasn't lost along the way to New Mexico, until I met Color.

"You can write anything. We won't judge you," Jesús says. "There's no judging in Heaven."

"That wouldn't be very heavenly of us," Color says.

But there are shadows. I can see mine, hanging over me and around me, cast not just on the walls, but everywhere. I can't seem to get away from them.

Color rattles the bucket of markers and holds it out. "Go for it."

I steal a glance at Moss. I don't know why, but I do. I want him to trust me. I remember what he said at the river. He runs because he's escaping something, too. Maybe we all are. But here in this place, maybe I can stop running. Maybe I can just . . . be.

If I want them to trust me, I have to trust them. And trust is handing over a piece of your heart to someone and believing they'll hold it as delicately as you do.

I take the bucket from Color and find a magenta marker. My head starts to swim as the blood goes to my toes again. I walk up to a blank space on the wall, and I take a breath so I don't fall over. I close my eyes and ask myself if this is OK. But it feels OK. It feels better than that. It feels like there's life in the desert after all.

And life begets life begets life begets life.

I write on the wall, adding my lost piece to Heaven, and in that moment, I actually pray it will be found. I ask the God that Tom believes in for the impossible. That's what he's supposed to do after all.

I ask that *she* will be found. If only for a moment. Just to see her eyes.

When I'm done, Jesús says, "What does *she* mean?" The boy who brought me back to life stands behind me, his arm touching mine.

What doesn't *she* mean?

I step back, wobbling on my feet because my blood isn't pumping right, and I haven't breathed in a while. It's happening again—I'm being chased by memories, and yet I'm paralyzed. My only choice is to let it wash over me.

"It's what the nurse called her," I say.

"Called who?" Moss says from across the room. I can't read his tone. He's a complex math problem, and I don't have time to solve it right now.

It really does feel like I'm in heaven here. Like I could be free. Like maybe I don't need to run.

"The baby," I say.

The bucket of markers falls from my hand with a heavy thud. Every color of the rainbow cascades onto Heaven's floor. This time, I don't have an empty pool to drown in or a pillow to cover me. The memory hits me like a wave, the feeling of being knocked over rocking me backward as I stand. I have to catch myself on the wall.

"It's a girl," the nurse said, protectively cradling a blanket. Somewhere inside it was a tiny baby, exposed just enough to haunt me forever.

"You promised I'd never know," I said to Mom.

"It was a mistake," Mom said. "The nurse made a mistake. It happens."

"She gets to keep her mistake. Why can't I keep mine?"

"You know why," Mom said. "This is the solution we came to."

"The solution," I said.

"To the problem, Esther."

But the baby didn't feel like a problem then. *She* felt like the answer.

10

Tom said I needed to ask for forgiveness, and God would give it to me. It was that easy. But God really wasn't in the forefront of my mind when it came to forgiveness. What about Mom and Hannah? Amit? And what about the baby? What about her? I *gave* her away. For the rest of her life, she'll know I did that. She'll paint a picture of me however she wants, just like I do with my scumbag dad. He gave Hannah and me away, and now, I've done the same. As if I didn't already have abandonment issues.

I don't need forgiveness from God. I need forgiveness from myself.

"Esther."

I blink with lazy eyes. My head swims through thick air.

"Esther. Are you OK?"

"Lay her down and put her feet up the wall," Jesús says.

"That's a terrible idea," Moss says.

"You have a better idea, Fungus?"

"Don't call me Fungus."

"Then don't act like one."

I can see and hear them talking, but I can't seem to respond. It's like my body has given out. I've carried this secret with me all the way from Ohio to New Mexico. Tom said I was leaving it behind, but that's not how secrets work. They follow you. Haunt you. Steal your breath when you're not looking.

"Google what to do when someone faints," Moss says. "Does she need mouth to mouth or something?"

"Don't be ridiculous," Jesús says.

"What's so ridiculous about that?"

"She's clearly breathing," Jesús says. "You just want to put your mouth on hers."

"Shut up, asshole."

"Whatever. I'm rubber. You're glue."

"You both are being butt heads," Color says.

The spots in my vision clear, and blood returns to my hands in tingles.

"I'm OK." I try to push myself up against the wall, but my arms are weak. I slump back onto my butt.

"Don't move." Moss puts his hand to my forehead. "You're cold."

"That's a first," I say.

Moss goes and gets a hat from the box of winter items Color took from my house. He puts my own hat on my head, and I cringe. It has a fluffy ball on top. I can't believe I almost fainted. How embarrassing.

Moss holds out the bag of chips. "Eat something."

But Jesús pushes him away. "I thought you didn't trust her."

Moss seems to remember this and backs away. "Fine."

"Don't worry, mon chéri. Jesús is here. I won't let you die." He pets my head.

"Stop being so dramatic," Moss says, pacing the other side of the room now. "She's not going to die."

"Telling me not to be dramatic is like asking a bird not to fly. I am who I am. Just like you are a fungus."

I pull the hat down on my head, shivers peppering my arms. "Moss is actually a plant," I say.

Both Moss and Jesús stare directly at me. Then Jesús laughs so loud the room feels brighter and lighter at the same time.

"Well, I'll be damned," Jesús says. "She just stuck up for you, Fungus."

"I think . . ." I look at the word I left on the wall. "I'm the one who's damned."

> Complex Math Problem: If four people are sitting in
> Heaven and a tsunami of truth floods them all, how
> many people survive?

I pull my hat down even farther, but it isn't big enough to cover me.

"You are not damned, Esther," Color says, sitting down next to me. Gently, she wraps her arm around my neck and hugs me to her. I close my eyes and wonder if she's telling the truth or just being nice.

"I can't believe you had a baby," Jesús says in my ear, as he snuggles up next to us. "Holy shit."

"That's one way to put it." I laugh. Reciprocal giggles echo through me, and it feels so good. Laughter changes everything. Amit taught me that.

"You're not . . ." I start to say.

"Not what?" Color pulls back with a confused look.

"Ashamed of me?"

"*Ashamed* of you?" When Jesús repeats the word, I cringe.

"Perfection is overrated," Color says. "What's the fun in that? It's our holes that make us interesting."

"It's a pretty big hole," I say.

"Well, it is now that you pushed a baby out of it," Jesús says. "But if what they tell us in Sex Ed is true, it goes back to the way it was. Don't worry." He pats my shoulder and gives me a wicked grin.

I catch Moss laying his nondescript gray eyes on me. He doesn't have to trust me. Half the time, I'm not sure I trust me. But he could stop looking at me that way—half intrigued and half wary that I'm even here. In defiance of his attitude, I say, "Now you know my biggest secret."

But Moss doesn't crack like I want him to. He stays securely whole, not allowing a single fissure for me to seep into and be a part of his life, like Color and Jesús did. He starts to collect all the markers on the ground, and when he's done he says, "I'm gonna go watch a movie."

Jesús helps me off the floor but doesn't let go, even when I'm steady and standing. "Ignore him. He likes black coffee. How boring."

I touch the word I wrote on the wall, just to make sure this is real. How did I end up here? Not just in Truth or Consequences—I know how that happened—but *here*. In this place with these people. It just feels like . . . magic.

It doesn't matter. I ask too many questions. It's going to get me in trouble someday. I'm here. And that's all that matters for now.

We make a plan to meet up at HuggaMug next week. Jesús says now that I've seen Heaven, he can no longer charge me for coffee. It just wouldn't be right, according to the laws of caffeine. Moss doesn't say anything. He just eats. He's moved on to Skittles, and his tongue has turned into a rainbow. I tell myself to stop looking at him and his tongue. It's a stupid tongue.

When Mom pulls up to the Blockbuster, I get into the front seat of the van, and she asks, "How was it?"

"Great."

She examines the boarded-up building. "What did you guys do at an empty Blockbuster? Nothing illegal, I hope."

"Nothing illegal," I say. A speck of magenta colors my fingertip. "Mom?"

"Yeah, Esther?"

"Do you ever think that heaven might be right here? Don't we say things at church like 'the kingdom of heaven here on earth'?"

"Heaven in Truth or Consequences?" Mom says with sarcasm. "God help us if that's the case."

11

When you've been to Heaven, it's hard to come back to earth, especially when tortured by the painful sobs of Fantine singing about the daughter she has to give away in *Les Misérables*. Hannah and Peter sit huddled on the couch, watching the musical's twenty-fifth anniversary special on PBS. When Hannah hears me walk into the room and sit down at the dining room table, she glances at me for a whisper of a moment before leaning into Peter. He grins and accepts the gesture. Our house is one of those open floor plans where every room leads into the next, and there are no doors except into bedrooms and bathrooms. It makes the emptiness worse. Beth told me last week that the air in a room can weigh up to one hundred pounds. Maybe that's why I feel so heavy when I'm in my house. All of that emptiness weighs a lot.

Hannah's Bible sits on the coffee table in front of her. For the past year, it's never been out of her reach. It's like I became pregnant, and Hannah became a Christian. I swear she does it to rub my sins in my face, but I'm pretty sure there's a commandment against that. Which leads to my theory that Hannah's Bible is Spanx, those things you wear underneath a dress to make you look skinnier. They suck you in and hold you in all the right places so it *looks* like you have really great curves. And then you take the Spanx off and stand naked in front of your mirror and what do you get? Reality. If I took that Bible away, I think Hannah would look quite different.

But I wouldn't do that, because the truth is, we all are wearing some version of Spanx.

Hannah glances over her shoulder at me like she's super annoyed that I'm even in the room. Hannah always cries when Fantine sings "I Dreamed a Dream." You'd think she'd have more compassion for me, considering Fantine turns into a prostitute and gives her kid away to Jean Valjean. I only had sex with Amit once . . . OK, maybe twice. OK, it was five times, I think. The first few times were kind of a mess. I'm not sure they count.

"Would you leave?" Hannah asks over her shoulder. "We're trying to watch TV, and your breathing is bothering me."

That's what our relationship has been reduced to? She's mad I'm *breathing* now?

"I want to watch, too."

Hannah huffs like she's a dragon, spewing fire all over the living room.

Do you ever read that Bible or do you just carry it around so it looks like you're reading it? I ask in my head. I don't dare say it aloud. She wouldn't answer even if I did.

I know I ruined her life. I know I'm the reason we had to move. I know that I don't deserve her love or friendship, but that doesn't mean I don't miss it. Before I cut my hair, Hannah was the one who always curled it for me. She'd get the back section, where I couldn't reach. That's what we did for each other. We saw the parts that the other person couldn't, and fixed them for each other.

But she couldn't fix my pregnancy. And I cut my hair. And I couldn't fix that Tom didn't want to live in a town where we were the center of gossip. Where every time I went outside, people stared. Where Mom couldn't go to the grocery store she worked at for eight years without being whispered about. Where Hannah, as an eighth grader, had to carry the shame of having a sister who not only had sex as a freshman, but got pregnant. Our town was so full of questions, it was hard to see.

Is she going to have the baby?
Is she going to give it up?
Is she going to abort it?
What must her parents think?
Is her life over?
What will she do now?
Who's the father?

I never told any of them about Amit. Not Mom or Tom or Hannah. He was and is my secret. Amit begged me to tell, and I begged him back not to.

"If you love me, you won't tell a soul," I said.

I ruined enough lives. I couldn't do that to him. And it turns out, Amit loved me a lot, because he kept our secret.

The only person who knows the truth about Amit is the baby. She is made up of him. She is the truth, but we gave her away because sometimes it isn't easy to look the truth in the eye. It's easier to run.

Mom, Tom, Hannah, and I—we ran. But for Hannah, it was more like she was dragged by her long auburn hair.

"What about me?" she yelled the night Tom made the decision to move us to Truth or Consequences, and Mom agreed to homeschool us. It wasn't the public school's fault. They had condoms available in the clinic. Amit and I just didn't get sick very often, so we weren't in there much. And I was too distracted by his eyes, and the way he hugged me, like he was healing me.

"Can you feel it?" he whispered once.

Yes. I could feel it. Amit was giving me love. I just forgot that people have to be careful with love. You can't go passing it back and forth to each other haphazardly, no matter how good it feels.

But I pushed Amit away along with his love. Hannah never cared about that, though.

"What about everything *I'm* losing?" she said one night, as the rain slashed on our windows and threatened to flatten our newly bloomed tulips.

I sat quietly on the couch as the baby hiccupped in my belly. She always got the hiccups at night.

"The high school is doing *West Side Story* next year. *West Side Story.* I was made to play Maria. Now I'll never get to play that role. I'll never even get to *go* to high school. I won't go to a dance or cheer at a football game or hold hands with a boy in the hallway while people watch. I was going to have everything, and you've ruined it. I have nothing now." Hannah talked about high school like it was *High School Musical.*

She stomped away, and I never said a word, because my words couldn't give her back what she lost. That and my belly kept bouncing as the baby hiccupped over and over.

Hannah lost the lead role in the high school production, and I lost a baby. I know I should feel bad for Hannah, but I can't. Sometimes I'll wake up in the middle of the night and think I still feel the baby hiccupping. I'll grab at my belly and realize that what once was full is now empty.

Hannah doesn't know what high school is like because she never got to live it. But I lived with a baby inside of me. I knew her. And I gave her away. I should feel bad for Hannah, but when I think about that, I can't.

I watch *Les Mis* with Hannah and Peter until Jean Valjean sings, "Bring Him Home," then I have to leave because I might cry.

Our words have made a maze of our friendship, and I'm starting to think there is no way back to the beginning. I go to my room, lie down on my bed, and stare at my fish.

"What's your name?" I ask it.

She doesn't respond, not that I expect her to.

12

Jesús balls up a piece of paper and throws it into the garbage with a grunt. I sit on the couch at HuggaMug, finishing my third iced soy mocha frap. My legs are shaking. It's awesome. I can't get enough. It's like I'm on speed. Legal speed. I might do something impulsive at any minute, because I'm so hopped up on caffeine I can barely stand it. My whole body seems to scream, *I love coffee!* Jesús is so right. It brings you back to life. I am so alive right now.

"What is it?" Color asks him. She's building a pyramid with to-go cups.

"Two words—'senior statement.'"

"Ugh." Color rolls her eyes dramatically.

"What's a senior statement?" I ask. My heart is pounding so hard my shirt is actually moving.

"It's like this stupid requirement all seniors have to do to graduate."

"Be glad you don't go to public school," Color says.

"I actually miss high school."

"Why? It's torture," Jesús says. "So many boys. So many boys who like girls."

Color adds a cup to the stack. "Just wait until college."

"I'm terrible at waiting," Jesús says. "I need someone to froth my wand while I'm young. Where's Moss when I need him? I've seen how he makes a latte."

I'm actually glad Moss isn't here. After the last time I saw him, I think avoidance might be the best option.

"Don't miss high school, Esther," Jesús says. "We're the coolest thing at school anyway, and you're already here with us."

"What's a senior statement?" I ask again.

"Oh, right. I have to write this ridiculous 'statement.'" Jesús makes air quotes. "About my 'truth.'" He makes air quotes again. "It's like a protestation of life as we see it upon leaving high school. It's supposed to"—he makes air quotes for a third time—"'help guide our futures.'"

"'That sucks.'" I put my words in air quotes because I'm high on caffeine, and it feels like it's a funny thing to do in my head. Jesús laughs, so maybe I'm right.

"I mean, I don't know what my truth is. And if this is living"—Jesús gestures around the shack—"working at a café that's really just an old converted toolshed—kill me now."

"What is truth anyway?" Color says, adding another cup to her pyramid. "It's too esoteric a question. I mean, what is *real*, really?"

"Don't go down this rabbit hole, Color." Jesús shakes his head.

"Seriously, maybe this is all just one big mirage. Maybe this isn't life at all. It's just a play in our minds. We're living in our mind's world, thinking it's really *the* world."

"This is some *Inception* kind of shit you're talking about," Jesús says. "Stop watching that movie."

"I love that movie," Color says with a smile.

"Help me, mon chéri." Jesús pretends to faint onto my lap. "Can I borrow your truth? No one will know."

"I'm hiding out in a coffee shack. I'm not sure I have a truth." My knees bounce and so does Jesús's head.

The bell rings, and Jesús gets up to take a customer's order.

"Welcome to HuggaMug; let me help you," he says through the window.

I wish I could help him. But I'm the girl who got pregnant and hid it, who kept Amit secretly locked in my heart for no one to know. The truth is clearly not my specialty.

Jesús makes a double dry espresso and hands it to the person in the car. He asks the driver, "Is this world just a mirage?"

I hear her respond, "Well . . . we *are* in the desert."

"You are a wise woman. Have a beautiful day." When she's gone, Jesús says, "She was no help."

"It's not due until the end of the year," Color says. "You have time to find your truth." Then her pyramid crumbles to the ground. She looks at me. "I knew it wouldn't last. Everything crumbles."

Color and Jesús pick up the fallen cups, but I'm so stuck on the couch in my geeked-out coffee haze that I can't get up. I don't know how I went fifteen years without this stuff. Life is simply better on coffee. That's the truth.

As Color and Jesús collect the to-go cups from the ground, they glance at me over their shoulders and whisper in hushed giggles.

"What?" I say, getting self-conscious. They giggle some more. *"What?"*

"We have a question for you," Jesús says.

"We covered this. I'm not great with answers."

"Oh, you know this answer," he says. And then they turn around, Color with two cups over her chest like gigantic boobs, and Jesús holding one over his crotch. He swings the cup around. "We want to know about sex."

"What?" I balk.

"Sex." Jesús pokes Color in the side with his penis cup.

"You mean, you haven't . . ."

Jesús puts the cup on his head now, like a crown, and walks toward me like a model. "Gay in a small town. Not happening anytime soon for me." The cup falls from his head, and he catches it.

I eye Color, and she shakes her head. "I need love first."

When she came to clean my house this week, Color told me more about her mom. How she was with their dad for two years, living in Scotland (hence Color's red hair) because she's a wanderer and can't stay still for very long, and how it was wonderful for a while, but then it all fell apart. Just like her cup pyramid.

Her dad still lives in Scotland, but her mom brought her and Moss back to the States. He sends money every now and then, which is more than my dad does, and she thinks someday she'll go overseas to visit him. And her mom still wanders. "She's like the river," Color said. "Always moving. My brother has a hard time with it. He's actually like moss. He gets attached to things." And the whole time Color was talking, I couldn't tell if she was mad at her mom, or sad, or understanding on some level, because Color's like a river, too.

Jesús kneels in front of me with big doe eyes and places his penis cup on my head.

"Tell us everything," he says.

I hold the cup out to him. "I might need more coffee for this."

Jesús makes me another iced soy mocha frap. I am never going to fit into the dress by Christmas, but I take a drink anyway, because fitting into a dress is overrated compared to coffee. At this point, I'd sacrifice a limb for my java.

"You mouthing that straw only makes the anticipation better," Jesús says. I swat him in the arm.

Swirling my drink around, I say, "I guess it's awkward at first."

"Did it hurt?" Color blurts out.

"A little . . . the first time . . . but then . . ."

Jesús grabs Color's hand. "This is the part I've been waiting for. Don't leave anything out."

I have to close my eyes, because the caffeine is going to my head and making me kind of loopy and light-headed. I liked having sex with Amit, but he and I were more than that.

"You're just so close to each other. It's like your body isn't your own anymore. You're sharing it with someone else. It's like your breath is his breath, and your heart is his heart. And there's a part of you that doesn't want to give it away because no one likes to lose things. But the closer you get . . ."

"Go on," Jesús says in a husky voice.

"You don't want to let go, because when you do, you know afterward you might feel a little more empty than you did before. But you do let go, because something inside of you knows it's OK to give a piece of yourself away. And in the end, if you love the person, even though you just gave a piece of yourself away, he handed a piece of himself right back to you."

"Did you love him?" Color asks.

For the first time, I say his name out loud. "Amit. And yeah, I think I did." Mom and Tom said I couldn't have loved anybody at my age, because I didn't know enough. But adults don't know love without strings attached. Amit and I were free.

"He sounds foreign and hot." Jesús fans himself. "Tell me more about him."

How do I share all the pieces of Amit? He was the opposite of every male I had ever met. He didn't want to control me like Tom, or make me love him and then leave me, like my dad. Amit was just there. Always. With no ulterior motive. I think simply being there is the most loving thing a person can do.

"He always carried an extra pencil just for me," I say. "I perpetually forgot mine. But I never had to ask to borrow one. Amit would merely hold out his hand, and what I needed would be there."

"I need an Amit in my life," Jesús says.

"So what happened to the baby?" Color asks in a soft voice.

"She was given up for adoption," I say. "I wasn't even allowed to see her."

"Not even for a second?" Jesús asks.

"It would have only made it harder." That's what Mom said, though now I find myself saying, "But . . ."

"But what?" Jesús asks and touches my leg. It's shaking, though I'm not sure it's from the coffee anymore.

"It's OK," Color says. "You can tell us, Esther."

"I'd just like to know what she looks like," I say. "Does she have Amit's eyes? He has really beautiful eyes."

The drive-through dings, a customer, but we don't move. I've never told anyone this. Never spoken about pencils and Amit and love so freely. I reserve those conversations for my memories. Presently, Jesús's hand is resting on my thigh. It feels nice.

"Hello?" the man in the car hollers through the window. "Hello, I see you in there!"

Hello, Esther, I see you in there. Come out. Is that what the universe is saying right now? And is it safe?

"I'd like a coffee!" the guy yells. "Black with two sugar packets!"

Jesús groans and goes to the window. "We're talking about love in here! Give us a moment!"

"But what about my coffee?"

Jesús starts pelting him with sugar packets. "Here! Take your sugar!"

"Asshole." The guy pulls away without his coffee.

"Wow," Color says. "My mom could learn something from Amit."

"Wow," Jesús says, sitting down next to me again. "I wish I could answer your questions about the baby, Esther."

I shrug. "Maybe this is all a dream, and I'll wake up in another reality tomorrow."

"What is tomorrow, anyway?" Color says. "Time is a mirage."

"I like that." Jesús gets a fresh piece of paper and writes that down. He puts his pencil in his mouth. "What else?"

"The better question is—Is a mirage really a mirage?"

"That's deep," Jesús says, scribbling.

"What's deep? Maybe deep is really shallow, and vice versa."

Jesús stops writing. "We've jumped into the rabbit hole again."

"Is a rabbit hole really a rabbit hole?" Color asks. "Is anything . . . anything?"

This, right here in HuggaMug, feels like something, so I say, "God, I hope so."

Moss walks in the side door then, startling us. He's dripping with sweat and in his running clothes. He takes his shirt and wipes the moisture from his forehead, allowing me to catch a glimpse of his stomach. Mine tightens. It's the coffee. It's the coffee. It's the coffee.

But I've felt this before—before I ever even drank coffee. Back when a classroom was a classroom and not my bedroom. Back when people shared pencils, along with love.

It's *so* not the coffee.

I hate to admit it, but the shorts look good on Moss.

"Sorry, I'm late," he says. "Practice went over."

"Some of us prefer to run through life. Some like to walk." Color points at the notebook. "Write that down."

"Good one," Jesús says.

Moss gets a glass of water. "What are you talking about?"

"The glass is half-full or half-empty, but is the glass really a glass?" Jesús says, still scribbling.

"Seriously, tell me," Moss says, disgruntled at being on the outside for once. Underneath his loose running shorts, he's wearing spandex shorts.

I blurt out, "Life is one big pair of Spanx. We squeeze to fit in. And if worn correctly, we can prevent chafing."

Jesus grins. "And I thought you said you'd be no help."

13

I sit at the bottom of our empty pool, a notebook in my lap, just in case I catch the truth and need to jot it down for Jesús, but all I'm catching right now is the scent of the past. Somewhere in Ohio a tree has turned from green to yellow to orange and red. The leaves dangle off their branches, holding on to life, barely.

That was me not long ago. It's hard to believe I have two people, Color and Jesús, I can grasp and yet, when the wind blows tonight, I smell rain-soaked fall leaves.

"Twelve weeks," the doctor said.

I pinch my nose closed and hold my breath, not wanting the memory to overtake me, but even suffocation can't save me. I'm pretty sure when I die, God will stand with a clipboard full of my sins, ready to tick them off, brutally replaying my life, moment by moment, as final punishment.

Giving in, surrendering, I exhale and let my mind be consumed, flooding me.

"I'm sorry. How far along?" Mom asked.

"Twelve weeks," the doctor said. "The baby has a strong heartbeat."

"Heartbeat," Mom repeated.

"Heartbeat," the doctor echoed. She pointed to the screen. That's the most I ever saw of the baby—a black-and-white mess, indiscernible to the untrained eye. "See. Right there."

"Twelve weeks," Mom said again. "What's the probability of miscarriage?"

"At this point, less than one percent. You have some very serious choices to make, Esther."

Amit would have offered his hand for me to hold. He would have placed a pencil in my palm so I could solve the problem. Mom moved in front of the ultrasound screen, blocking my view, and put the adoption information in her purse.

"I'll take care of this," she said.

I rest my hands on my lower belly, wondering if I can feel the baby's heartbeat still inside of me.

Nothing.

∞

Forget avoidance. It is completely overrated. Fine if you want to avoid the plague, but Moss has no reason not to trust me. That's why I'm hiding in the bushes, fully prepared to jump out at him when he comes running by.

This tactic might not be the most solid I've come up with to date, but he won't even look at me when we're around Jesús and Color.

Why?

But I know the answer. Moss knows I'm hiding things. I hide things under my bed. I'm hiding from the past. I'm even hiding in the bushes.

But the truth is—Moss is the missing piece. I need him to like me. Color and Jesús do, and he's a part of the group.

OK. That's not the whole truth, and I know it.

"Because maybe I like him," I whisper to the air. "And his running shorts." It's the feeling I get in my stomach. The drop. The roller coaster. I haven't felt that in a long time.

When I hear the familiar sound of Moss's shoes on the pavement, I jump out and shock him so badly that he trips off the side of the path and almost falls in the river. I have to grab his arm to stop him.

He shakes me off immediately. "I'd say thank you, but you almost just killed me!" Moss heaves and puts his hands on his hips. "Why do you always do that?"

"What?"

"Jump out at me!"

"It's the only way to get your attention." I shrug.

"You're delusional." He starts down the path, but I'm quick on my bike, following him closely.

"Practicing for cross-country again?" I ride right behind him. "I assume."

"You assume right. Good for you." His gaze stays trained on the path.

"Where's the rest of the team?"

"What?"

"Aren't you supposed to run with, like, people?"

Moss keeps trudging along, as if his feet are lightweight, almost buoyant. "I prefer to run alone. As long as I get my miles in, Coach doesn't care."

"Isn't that kind of boring?"

"Did you hear me when I said I prefer it?"

His attitude sucks. I know I jumped out at him, but come on, I'm trying.

"Fine," I say, slowing down.

"Fine," he says, picking up the pace. But stubbornness gets the better of me almost instantly. This is my path, too. He doesn't own it. I ride faster to catch up to him.

"Why do you prefer to be by yourself?" I ask.

"I can think better that way," he hollers, and I'm surprised when I feel sympathy. I get the need to think. It's why I lie in the empty pool.

"About what?"

Moss stops on the trail. "Stuff," he says.

"Stuff?"

"Yeah, stuff."

I watch him sweat and breathe. His eyes look like storm clouds. Just like Color. And I want to be in his head so badly. Yes, his body is in quite fine shape, but nothing is more intimate and sexy than when a person takes you on a walk through his thoughts. "What's your truth?" I ask.

"Huh?"

"Jesús is writing his senior statement about his truth. What's yours?"

Moss starts running again, and I follow him. Again. "I've got another year to think about it. I'll let you know when I'm a senior." And then Moss stops. He has to grab my handlebars to prevent a collision. "Look, why are you doing this?"

"Because you said you don't trust me. I want to prove to you that you can."

"By chasing me on your bike? That's messed up."

The words sting, because he's right. I don't know what I was thinking. This is clearly not working. Moss doesn't want me in his head. He doesn't want to get to know me either. Every question I ask is a dead end.

"I just wanted to say that I get it."

"Get what?" he asks sharply.

Color said Moss is like moss. He gets attached. Or maybe he's stuck, and he wants a way out. That's why he runs.

"Never mind. I just thought you might like some company. I was wrong."

This is the point where I should turn and ride away, but actually doing that is harder than knowing it should be done. Moss exhales loudly through his nose, eyes on the ground. Sweat collects in a small puddle there. Begrudgingly, I start to turn my bike in the other direction.

"Wait," he says. "Can you be quiet?"

I show that I can by squeezing my lips tightly together.

"Can you stay off my heels?"

"I'll be practically invisible."

"No more jumping out of bushes."

"OK."

Moss starts running again, and I think I hear him say, "And I don't want you to be invisible." But I could have just heard what I wanted to hear.

∞

Heaven is just as good the second time. I stand in front of the wall of lost family pictures. Jesús sits on one of the oversized chairs, supposedly working on his senior statement, but really he's taking a nap. Moss is MIA, and I try not to care.

Color comes to stand next to me. She's wearing one of my winter hats. It looks better on her, her red curls peeking out from underneath.

"Sometimes when I'm really mad at my mom, I'll look at these pictures and try to imagine myself with another family. What would it be like to live with these people?" Color picks up a family picture with everyone wearing matching outfits of khaki pants and white button-down shirts.

"No way," I say to her.

Color agrees and picks up a picture of a family wearing Pittsburgh Steelers football jerseys. I shake my head, and Color gags herself.

"Or this one." She pulls a picture gently from the pile. The parents are in the background. Three kids, all with black hair, are caught jumping in a gigantic leaf pile. Everyone looks so happy, it almost breaks my heart.

"Closer," I say.

"I like this family," Color says. "They're my favorite." The look she gives the picture is like she's begging it to come alive, or like she's begging to see herself half-buried, next to the other kids, among the leaves. "But it's just a picture, right? It isn't reality."

"Is a picture really a picture?" I ask, and she laughs.

"My mom says that souls travel in packs," Color says, setting the picture down.

"Really?"

Color says, "Like a soul posse or something."

"A soul posse," I say.

"This soul posse . . ." She holds up the family picture again. "They seem cool."

A sinking feeling suddenly overtakes my stomach. It's so bad that I actually grab myself around the waist.

"What is it?" Color asks.

I might throw up. I know I've contemplated this truth before, somewhere in the back of my mind, but I hid it, like the boxes in my room. But now it's back, like my memories that creep up at times, overwhelming me with their vividness. Color did say everything crumbles. Well, the walls I built around this reality are tumbling down at this very moment.

I hear the question in my head, but this time I say it out loud, too. "What if the baby is in my soul posse, and I gave her away?" I didn't even get to touch her, let alone look at her. I don't know anything about her. She was taken like the wind takes a feather, pulled, tossed, and placed far away from me.

Color looks at me with kind eyes, or maybe sad eyes.

Complex Math Problem: If souls really do travel in groups, but one is subtracted, is she lost forever?

Did I ruin *her* life before it ever even started? Will she always feel lost and never really know why? I know the pain of looking in the mirror and wondering how someone who carries your genes, who made you, could just disappear, knowing they'd left pieces of their reflection behind.

It's quiet in Heaven. We let my question mingle with the other lost words on the walls. This may be how it is forever. My questions unrequited, like a lover waiting a lifetime for its other half.

And then Color lights up and says, "I think I have a way we can get you an answer, Esther."

14

Color knows exactly who we can go see. It's simple. She tells Jesús and me about her idea, stating evenly that it's easy. But it's not that simple or easy or perfect. Nothing ever is. Simple is an illusion. Even single-digit numbers are made up of infinite parts.

"Dharma is my mom's psychic. She swears by her," Color says. "She lives in Albuquerque. We'll go and ask her. It's that simple."

"That simple," I repeat, unconvinced. "How is a psychic going to help?"

"Dharma can give you the answer. She's like a doctor for your soul. She looks inside you, sees what's wrong, and tells you how to fix it. It's perfect." Color claps her hands in excitement.

"Does this doctor give physical exams, too," Jesús says, "because I'd like one of those."

Albuquerque is two hours away, which means we need an entire day to do this. It's one thing to sneak off for a couple hours here and there to see my friends, while Mom pretends I'm at the movies. It's another to go to a different city for the day to see a psychic. The only psychic Tom believes in is God, and I'm pretty sure I don't need a psychic to tell me how that one goes.

And then there's the fact that we all ride bikes. I don't need a complex math problem to figure out how long it will take two teens, one completely out of shape, to ride bikes one hundred and fifty miles.

A long damn time. I'll be living in hell before we ever even make it, dragged to hell by Tom.

"How are we going to get there?" I ask. "I don't have a license. Tom practically had a heart attack when I brought it up on my sixteenth birthday."

Color looks at Jesús.

"You know I don't have my license." He shrugs. "Some people were born to drive, some people were born to be driven."

"Moss," Color says. "He'll drive." She says this like it's no big deal.

"Moss doesn't like me."

"Mon chéri," Jesús says. "It's super easy to dislike people. Life is much more complicated when you can't figure out why you *like* someone. And Moss is very complicated. You catch my drift? I mean, we all thought he was a fungus until you pointed out he's actually a plant."

"But we don't have a car," I say.

"We do," Color says, and then she kind of bobbles her head as if not completely convinced of her own statement. "Well . . . I don't know if you would call it a car. I'm not entirely sure it's street legal. But whatever. Mom left it in case of emergencies. This is *so* an emergency."

"Oh my God, the old station wagon," Jesús says. "I haven't thought about that car in forever."

"You have a station wagon?" I ask.

"It's actually our granny's, but she's not driving it any time soon." Color puts her finger to her chin. "It might actually be our great-grandma's."

"Oh my God, road trip!" Jesús says. "This is the best idea you've had in a long time, Color."

"Thank you." She curtsies.

Color starts to buzz with plans. Her energy spreads through the whole room. For the first time since I gave the baby away, I feel like maybe everything isn't lost, like maybe putting her word on the wall in Heaven gave her a way to be found. Maybe I didn't move to New Mexico to get away from her. Maybe I moved here to get closer to her.

My head spins, unable to wrap around the idea that this could really happen.

"You would do this for me?" I ask.

Color just says, "Duh," like it's that simple, but again, a nugget of discomfort lodges itself in my throat. Nothing is simple.

"I get shotgun," Jesús says as he takes off toward the door. I stop him before he gets too far. And this has officially gone too far. For the past few minutes, I've envisioned us crammed in a station wagon, smiling, wind in our hair, free, but that truth doesn't exist for me.

"There's no way I'll be allowed to do this," I finally say. "There's no way Tom will let me go."

Jesús touches my arm. "There is no way you *can't* do this, mon chéri."

"There's always a way," Color says. "The universe is speaking to you, Esther, and we need to listen, or else."

"Or else what?" I ask.

"She'll start to scream. The universe does not like to be ignored."

"The universe sounds like Tom."

Complex Math Problem: If two opposing forces are pulling a whole person in different directions, will the result inevitably be a broken, fractional mess?

If I do what Tom wants of me, my past may haunt me forever, but if I listen to the universe, Tom might haunt my future indefinitely.

"Don't worry." Color hugs me tightly. "The universe never says anything it doesn't mean." And then her finger is up in the air. "Truth—the universe is always speaking, but people are too consumed with their own voices to hear her."

15

The gray-haired pet store guy watches me as I look through different items to decorate my fish tank. I've decided not everything around me needs to be dying. Not if I can help it. My fish deserves to be surrounded by more life. I pick up a plastic plant and think this might work.

"Any luck getting to California?"

"Not yet," I say. "Right now, I'm just trying to get to Albuquerque."

"Albuquerque? What's there?"

The colorful rocks look like a nice additive. Everyone and everything needs more color to feel alive. "Answers," I say. "And psychics."

"I called one of those psychic hotlines once. Huge mistake."

"Why?"

The guy behind the counter scratches his head. "I didn't need to pay a dollar ninety-nine a minute to have some lady tell me I'm a loser."

"But was she right?" I ask. "Did she answer your questions?"

The guy shrugs. "Yeah. I just didn't like what she said. But I guess that's the risk you take." Then he asks, "What's in California then?"

It's really none of his business, so I don't tell him. I set the plastic plant down and settle on the colorful rocks.

"Well, who will watch your fish when you go?"

"I'll set her free by then."

"It's a girl fish?"

"Yes." I hand him money for the rocks.

"You're gonna set her free? After all of this?" he says. "After months of taking care of her? Spending money?"

"That's been the plan all along," I say.

"Why not just do it then? Save yourself the time and effort."

I take my change and my decorations. "I'm just not ready to let go yet."

∞

Complex Math Problem: One plus one equals two.
What happens if you're a two, but you don't know the
ones who made you?

Our family picture sits on the mantel of the fireplace in the living room. I'm already living in a kiln, and my house has a fireplace. Tom says it's an accent piece. It's not there to work, but to look good. What Tom doesn't know is that *he's* the accent piece of this family, expertly picked by Mom from a Christian dating site. I knew she was lonely when Hannah and I were younger, but I didn't realize how completely loneliness turned to desperation for her. And desperate people are willing to overlook things to get what they need. Mom's pretty good at that.

"People are package deals, Esther." Those were Mom's words. Even when I glance at the sunshine coming in the window today, I see rain lashing outside, Mom at our old kitchen table, a glass of wine in front of her. I watched the drips run down the windows and melt holes in the snow.

Mom took a gulp of her wine. The glass was only half-full. One more sip and it would be half-empty.

"Sometimes you don't like everything in the package, but you deal with it because for the most part, it's good. Tom is a good man. And one day, you'll find a good man, too. That's why I'm doing this."

"So I can find a good man?" I asked.

"No. So your package isn't completely damaged." Mom pointed at my round belly. Even now as I look down, knowing nothing is in there, I think I feel the baby kick, like a phantom limb that once was a part of me, but was tragically removed. "This is not your future," Mom said. "You can start over."

I think what Mom really wanted to say was that this was not *her* future. That's why she married Tom in the first place. That's why she puts up with his bullshit. So the future wouldn't be as shitty as the past.

I pick a family photo off the mantel in our house in New Mexico and touch the Esther who stares back at me, a fake smile plastered on her face. It was taken a little over a year ago. We're different now, for a lot of reasons, but the most important one is that underneath the pressed and ironed clothes and the posed body, a baby had attached herself to me. No one but me knew this when the picture was taken. Her heart was beating, and her body was growing, along with mine.

I touch my abdomen again, relieved of the weight it carried for nine months. Sometimes when the wind blows fast and hard through the desert, I hear the empty pieces of myself, whistling.

"Do you need me to find you so you won't be lost forever?" I ask the old Esther. "Or maybe . . . Do I need to find you so I won't be lost forever?"

Is this about me or the baby? As I stare at the picture of myself, I'm not sure I can detach one from the other. After all, she is a piece of me.

Mom knew the baby was a part of her, too. That's the thing with women—we're all attached by the pure science of our reproductive systems. The egg that made me was in my mom, and after I was conceived, little eggs formed in my small ovaries, and *she* was there, years before she was ever born, a piece of her inside an unborn baby, who was living inside another person.

I'm pretty sure that's why Mom said what she did the night the rain melted the snow and she got drunk on a bottle of wine. When life feels so complex that nothing makes sense, the truth we bury sneaks out.

"Tell me what an axiom is," Mom said.

"A statement accepted as true without proof."

"You want to know what God is, Esther. God is an axiom." A little wine dribbled down her chin, and Mom used the back of her hand to wipe it up.

"What does that have to do anything?"

Mom exhaled, exhausted. I didn't blame her. "I don't know. Everything I thought I knew, I don't. Life has surprised me, Esther. I guess I have the Axiom to thank." She leaned on the table, her eyes dropping. "How are we supposed to accept something as truth if it can't be proved?"

"I think it's called faith," I said.

"Some people would call that bullshit." Mom sat up quickly and collected herself. "Don't tell Tom I said that."

Then she started crying. Her tears dripped on the papers she was protecting from my sight.

"I thought I lost you," she said. "When I was seven weeks pregnant, I started bleeding, and I thought for sure I was having a miscarriage. I called your grandma, frantic and frightened out of my mind. And you know what she said to me?"

I shook my head.

"She told me to get used to it. She told me that being a parent meant being perpetually afraid that something might happen to the one thing you don't want to lose. That every day you'll worry and think about this possibility to the point of madness, until all that's left is to throw your hands up and have faith that it's all going to be OK." Mom shook her head. "We have enough to worry about, Esther. I'm doing this to spare you that feeling. You're too young."

"But what about throwing your hands up and having faith?" I asked.

"Faith and bullshit wear the same clothes. It's impossible to know which is which."

I sit at our kitchen table in New Mexico, surrounded by beige walls, still clutching our family picture. Across from me sits the memory of Mom and her near-empty glass of wine. She's exhausted. She's unraveling like a piece of rope cut from the bundle.

"California," Mom said.

With my eyes on my belly in the family picture, I whisper, "Mom sent you to California. That's not fair."

Mom's response whispers across the table to me, as vivid today as it was months ago. "God the Axiom doesn't seem to care about fair, or dads wouldn't run off in the middle of the night and leave their babies behind."

"But California?" I begged her.

"Don't ask me any more, Esther," Mom said. "I hate lying, but I'll do it if it means protecting the one thing I can't lose."

I set the picture back on the mantel.

I guess lying to protect something that's important to you, something you can't let go of, is acceptable.

Maybe I should let lies carry me all the way to Albuquerque.

16

The car won't start. We stand in the garage at Color's house as she tries to turn over the engine. Her house is the opposite of mine. Whereas the front lawn at my house is a groomed patch of dead grass that Tom has professionally mowed every other week, Color's lawn is overgrown with weeds and tall grass and thistles. Color says she can't bring herself to kill anything, even the dandelions. Tom, on the other hand, doesn't water our grass because our water bill is so high. He's paying for *tidy* dead grass.

And an axiom is truth and truth is an axiom, but everything still remains unproved, which makes things really complicated.

I wish I lived at Color's house.

The base of the station wagon is covered in rust, and the tailpipe practically drags on the ground. A dead animal smell comes from somewhere inside the car. That can't be a good sign.

Color bangs the steering wheel. "Damn it."

"I don't think hitting it is going to work," Jesús says, petting the hood. "Give it some love."

That's when the car officially dies a bad death of smoke and exhaust and old age.

"Thank goodness we haven't had an emergency until now," Color says, waving smoke from her face as we walk out of the garage. "This is so symbolic. You think something is there to save you, but it turns out it's broken, just like you are."

"Maybe this is a sign," I say.

"It's just a sign that we need to go in a different direction." Color wraps her arm around me.

"And what direction is that?" I ask.

Color doesn't offer an answer. We walk into her house, a mess of dirty dishes in the sink, mail piled up. Most look like bills that probably need to be paid. But I get it. If I cleaned houses as an after-school job, I wouldn't want to come home and clean more.

"Don't worry. We'll figure it out," she says eventually. "There is always another way, or the universe wouldn't have created a right and left side."

I've never met anyone more confusing and brilliant at the same time.

"I could steal a car," Jesús says, taking cookies out of the pantry.

"No," I say. He offers me a chocolate chip cookie and winks.

As we drown our sorrow in sugar, Moss comes down the stairs to find us huddled in contemplation.

"What were you doing in your room?" Jesús wiggles his eyebrows at him.

"Nothing."

"Do you need any help doing . . . nothing?" Jesús blows him a kiss.

"Shut up."

"Your angst only makes you hotter."

Moss groans and rubs his buzzed head. "I'm going for a run. I'll make dinner when I get back."

Color says, "These walls are getting to me. I can't think. Let's put some more stars on my ceiling."

Color's room is just as messy as the downstairs, with clothes strewn all over the place. Even her underwear. The bed is only partially made, and a real mini evergreen tree sits potted in the corner, decorated with twinkle lights. Her ceiling is so star covered, you'd think she captured the Milky Way and painted it there.

With a fresh pack of glow-in-the-dark stickers, Color jumps up and down on her bed, adding more stars to her galaxy. I lie on the ground, staring up at her.

Jesús puts on one of Color's dresses and a bra he picks off the ground. He holds his arms out wide and spins.

"Do you think Brett would be convinced?" Jesús asks.

Color grabs Jesús in his nether region. "It's a hard sell."

"Well, it is now that you touched it." Jesús crosses his legs and sits down on the ground.

"I can't imagine having a penis," Color says. "All that stuff between your legs. It must just get in the way." She jumps and puts another glow-in-the-dark star on the ceiling. "And it's just so hard all the time. It's like walking around with an extra arm in an uncomfortable place."

"It's really hard that much?" I ask.

"More than I'd like to admit," Jesús says with a wicked grin. "You don't want your third arm coming out at the wrong time. Scares people off."

Moss sticks his head back in the room. "I'm leaving soon."

"We were just talking about touching penises. Interested, Fungus?" Jesús asks.

Moss glances at me for a second. I catch the unreadable look he's so good at producing and feel my face melt into an embarrassed expression. My stomach goes on another roller coaster ride. Damn it. It seems that Moss could gaze at me in any way—mad, sad, angry, disgusted— and all I'd want to do is touch his perfectly plump lips. He forces his eyes back to Jesús. "That dress looks hideous on you." Moss walks away and shuts the door.

Jesús examines himself in the mirror. "He's right. I'm not meant for drag."

"We're all in some form of drag," Color says.

"Ooh, can I use that for my senior statement?" he asks.

"What's mine is yours."

Jesús flops back onto the ground and groans. "I might never come up with anything for this stupid senior statement."

I understand his frustration. The truth is hard to find. It likes to hide, shifting shape, and depending on who finds it first, they can remold it anyway they want.

I get up, telling Jesús and Color that I have to use the bathroom, even though I don't have to go at all. I just want to poke around for Moss and his lips, instead of lying there feeling lost. I really want to dislike Moss. I want to not care. But then all of a sudden, *he'll* care for just a moment, and it jumbles me up. It's obvious how much he loves Color, how he takes care of her. And even Jesús, despite all their jabbing back and forth. The words might be sharp, but the tone . . . there's love there somewhere. Love is the sexiest thing I've ever seen. And it all just gives me hope for something . . . more. Hope that maybe I can embrace love again.

I stop outside his bedroom where the door is partially open. Nothing is on the floor. The bed is made, and a map of the world hangs on the wall, with red tacks all over it.

I take a step closer and catch Moss getting dressed. He's shirtless and pulling his shorts up over his boxer briefs. I can see the outline of his butt and his muscular legs. The human body is pretty sexy, too, especially when covered in lean muscle.

My stomach rolls over and inside out. I bite my bottom lip and know I should turn away. Walk away. Get the hell away from this scene, but I can't. I watch as he sits down on the end of his bed and ties his shoes. He runs his hand over his buzzed head and exhales. He lets go of his breath as if he's tired. Tired of what, I don't know. He barely speaks. And why run so much if he's so tired? Though I think I know that answer. Sometimes letting yourself be consumed by feelings is scary. We'd rather engage in a fistfight, knowing we'll accumulate some bruises, in an effort to avoid the internal scarring that hurts more. As if Moss is in my head, he stands up and jumps up and down, like he's getting ready to fight someone. Or something.

> Complex Math Problem: If you punch a cloud, will the cloud split into fragments, or will you? In other words—If your enemy is invisible, who breaks into fractions when you throw a punch? Would it just be easier to preserve the whole and surrender?

Moss pulls open his bedroom door wider, quicker than I have time to move, and nearly runs into me.

"What do you want?" he asks as we stumble back from each other.

"I was just . . . looking . . ."

"Looking?"

I point at the map on the wall. "The tacks on your map . . . what are they for?"

His lips stay tight. My mouth is so dry I can barely talk. Damn the desert.

"I'm leaving now," he says, walking past me.

"Will you ride me home?" I ask quickly.

"Ride you home?" he says sarcastically.

I bite my tongue and swallow the little bit of spit in my mouth. "It's getting dark, and I rode my bike here. I thought maybe you could run next to me? To make sure I get home safely. I know it's not the path along the river, but . . ."

Moss rubs his head, eyes on anything but me. I feel like an idiot. He caught me snooping and staring. He has really nice legs and arms. And then I find myself thinking about his third arm, and all the muscles all over his body, and how it might be nice to be surrounded by all of that muscle, hugged close to him, so maybe I could feel the love he has inside that he doesn't want to show. My face heats uncontrollably.

"Never mind. I'll be fine," I say and start to walk away.

Moss stops me. "I'll do it. Meet me downstairs."

Anywhere. I'd meet Moss anywhere. But I don't say that.

When I go back into Color's room to say goodbye, she and Jesús are sitting on the floor in the dark, staring up at the glow-in-the-dark stars. It looks like an illuminated night sky.

"It's just like being outside," Color says in awe. "No crumbling walls."

A moment passes in silence.

And then Jesús says, "We can pretend, at least."

"Yes we can," Color says. She exhales sadly, and I remember we're in a house that's missing a parent.

I don't let the heartbreaking moment linger for long before I tell them I need to go.

"Don't worry, Esther. It's going to happen for you." Color hands me my very own pack of glow-in-the-dark stars, and winks. "That's the truth. I can feel it."

"Will you feel me, too?" Jesús says, and takes Color's hand and puts it on his crotch. She shoves him in the arm, and I leave them in a sea of laughter that, for the moment, washes away the sadness.

Moss runs next to me as I bike through Truth or Consequences on my way home. We don't say a word. He just keeps pace with me, his eyes on the road ahead of him. When we get to my street, I tell Moss I'm OK. That I can make it home from here. Mom and Tom would flip if they saw me with a boy. He agrees and turns to go.

"Wait." When I touch his arm, he tenses under my fingers, but almost immediately relaxes. I keep my hand on him, because why not. I'm already here. "You know what's odd, Moss?"

"What?"

I smile. "Every other number."

"That's a terrible joke," he says, shaking his head. But he laughs anyway. It's just a light giggle . . . but it feels real. That's when I decide to let him go.

17

Something is missing. It's a feeling I get in the middle of the night when I'm dreaming. I'll wake up and grab at my stomach and think she's still there. I'll feel around for her, touching my belly, and all I find is loose flesh.

And off in the distance, I think I hear a baby cry.

It's just my imagination, but sometimes what we pretend hurts more than reality.

"Hey, Esther, when you smile, you look like a thirty-degree angle," Amit whispers.

"I do?" I whisper back.

"Yeah, because you sure are acute-y." He looks at me with golden eyes. He's nervous, I can tell. He was always nervous. His eyes are flooded with shyness, which only makes him cuter, because vulnerability is sexy, like love is. It's as if Amit is asking permission—permission to love me.

As I lie in bed, two perfectly round flecks of gold reflect on my blank ceiling.

"Actually, you're a whole number, Esther," Amit says. "Nothing is missing."

At that, I can't help but cradle his hand in mine. Permission granted.

When I get the courage to look at my hand, lying vacant on the bed next to me, I can't stand being inside my dry, static-ridden house, so I head out to the pool, where the gold flecks of Amit's eyes can get lost in the stars.

Will this ever go away? I ask the sky.

It responds with only the echo of wind rushing down the street.

∞

Today Beth is wearing a shirt that says:

AND GOD SAID

DIV $\mathbf{B} = \mathbf{0}$

DIV $\mathbf{D} = \rho_v$

ROT $\mathbf{E} = -\partial\mathbf{B}/\partial t$

ROT $\mathbf{H} = \mathbf{j} + \partial\mathbf{D}/\partial t$

AND THEN THERE WAS LIGHT.

Here are a few notable things about Beth. She's full of weird facts. She clearly hates Pastor Rick. She wears interesting T-shirts. She's smart. She always saves me a seat. She grasps her cross necklace like it's a life preserver thrown over the edge of a boat to save her from drowning in a raging sea of sins, and *that* scares me.

There is no way I can tell her I had a baby out of wedlock. Beth might die. She might keel over, drowning in *my* sins, still holding on to her cross, and meet Jesus face-to-face. They'd both be shaking their heads.

But then there's her shirt and her general attitude for Pastor Rick, who loves Christ, too. Aren't they on the same team? Singing the same tune? Shouldn't they get along, for Christ's sake?

"What does your shirt mean?" I ask as I sit down.

Beth examines it. "It's physics. Maxwell's equations for electromagnetism." I look at her blankly, and she adds, "It's a science joke."

"God didn't create light?" I ask.

"Who said God and science have to be mutually exclusive?" Beth starts grabbing at her necklace again. Sweet, electrifying Jesus.

"Um, like everyone at this church," I say.

"Think about it," Beth says. She squares herself to me, getting more animated. "Why can't God be science and science be God? Why do they have to function apart from each other?"

"I don't know," I say.

"Think about the math problem I gave you. What's the answer?"

"Point nine recurring is equal to one."

Beth nudges me in the shoulder a little harder than I expect, which only makes me like her more. "Yes. If that isn't proof there is a God, I don't know what is."

I am so lost right now, I can't even remember where I started. "How do you figure?"

"Infinity exists in the whole," Beth says, her arms moving to emphasize each of the words. "You can be infinite and finite at the same time. You're born and you die. Finite. But there's a part of you, your soul, that has always existed, so it was never born, and it can never die. Infinite. It's so freaking mind-blowing. Only God could think of that."

> Complex Math Problem: If .9 recurring is indeed equal to 1, does that mean Beth is more complicated than I thought?

"Sorry," Beth says, sitting back in her seat. "I geek out over this stuff."

Have I assumed Beth is one solid number, without remembering that each number has its own unique qualities? I haven't spent the time to investigate Beth because I've judged her by her outside instead of dissecting her parts.

And then she's upright and excited again; her hand gestures in full force. "Get this—a cumulous cloud weighs over eight hundred pounds. And it floats in the air! I mean, what?! If I drilled a hole right through the earth, you could jump through and be on the other side of the planet in just over forty-two minutes. That's freaking crazy!"

"That *is* crazy."

"It's all just so beyond our grasp." Beth shakes her head. "There just has to be a God."

Beth pulls on her necklace, moving the cross back and forth across her neck. Since Beth is full of interesting facts, I decide to ask the question I've been pondering ever since I sat down next to her at our first choir practice.

"Who gave you the necklace?" I ask. "It's clearly important to you. You're always wearing it."

She looks down at the gold cross, and her face paints with a blush. "My first love."

I almost fall out of my chair. Like, for real. "You've been in love?" I say it a little too loud, and Beth looks around the room, her blush deepening. I lean in protectively and whisper, "What's his name?"

Beth whispers back, "Brittany."

∞

Here is a notable thing about Beth. She is not who I thought she was.

Ms. Sylvia taps her wand thing on the choir stand, directing us to start singing the Smashing Pumpkins version of "Christmastime." And Beth just sings, like she didn't just drop a sinner-sized bomb in my lap. I'm literally exploding right now.

When the song ends and I haven't sung a single note, I lean in and whisper, "You're gay? Do people at church know?"

Beth whispers back. "Only five people know."

"Who?"

"My mom, my dad, Brittany." Beth glances at me. "You."

"And . . ."

"God."

I explode again, barely able to contain myself, but this time it's laced with guilt. She just told me her truth. She trusts me and here I am, a walking and talking jumble of secrets, and I haven't told her anything. I suck.

"You trust me with your secret?"

"It's not a secret, Esther. It's *me*," she says.

And I feel like I *see* Beth, like really see her, for the first time. The truth looks beautiful on her. Truth is like love—it's sexy. Beth is stunning.

Ms. Sylvia tells us to get out our sheet music for Dido's "Christmas Day." Beth rolls her eyes. "This isn't even a Christian song. What the fuck."

Halfway through the song, as I'm trying to concentrate on reading the notes and lyrics, but really wanting to hear more about beautiful Beth, Pastor Rick walks through the door in his hooded sweatshirt and messy hair. The room falls into quiet silence and ogling eyes. Beth sits back in her chair and crosses her arms over her chest.

"I want to punch him in his perfect face." Beth glares. "Then he wouldn't look so . . . perfect."

Pastor Rick announces that Touchdown Church will host a "Thanksgiving Youth Service Day" on Sunday, and he hopes all the *awesome* youths in the room will participate. He goes through the options for the day—carol singing at the retirement home, working the coat drive at the church, sorting donated cans, and delivering turkeys to the needy in and around Truth or Consequences.

Clipboards are passed around the room for sign-ups. When it gets to Beth and me, I notice Hannah has signed up to sing at the retirement community. Peter's name is directly underneath hers. Last Sunday, I found them after church in the choir room, singing "One Hand, One Heart" from *West Side Story*, cuddled up in each other's arms.

"We should do the turkeys," Beth says. "Then we won't be stuck here all day."

I point to the asterisk at the top of the page. "It says you need a car."

"No big deal. I'll borrow my parents'."

When Beth says that, my head gets light, and I almost burst into a million honest pieces all over our ridiculous sheet music. I think the universe just spoke through Beth.

"Hey, Beth?"

"Yeah, Esther?" Her necklace sparkles in the light of the room.

"What does science say about psychics?"

18

Hannah comes into my room, carrying an open box. I'm jumping on the bed, putting the glow-in-the-dark stars Color gave me on the ceiling.

I stop, out of breath, as Hannah sets the box down on the bed.

"What are you doing?"

"Jumping on the bed," I say.

Hannah gives me a look that screams, *You're so weird, Esther!*

I sit down. "What do you want, Hannah?"

She looks around at my clean room. "When did you become a neat freak?" And again Hannah's tone is judgmental, but at the core it also sounds kind of sad. Like Hannah is really asking, *How did we grow so far apart that you could transform from a messy person into a neat freak right under my nose?* But I don't keep my room clean for me. I keep it clean for Color, so she doesn't have to work so hard. And I'm not about to tell Hannah that. Plus, it's not really clean. I'm just hiding my mess. It's still there under the bed and in the closet.

"I don't know," I say.

Hannah walks over and squats down in front of the fishbowl. "How's your fish?" She taps on the glass and my fish jumps, scared.

"Please don't do that."

"Sorry," she says softly, like she means it.

This whole moment is weird—Hannah in my room, asking me questions. It's like she's here to find something, but she won't come out and say it. The saddest part of all is that I don't trust her. I don't want Hannah to find whatever she's looking for. I just want her to get out of my room.

Instead, she sits down on my bed. "Do you think Tom will ever fill the pool?"

"I don't know," I say.

"Well . . . do you like living here?"

"I don't know." I cross my arms over my chest. I'm a one-response parrot. But I really don't know what to say to Hannah. She literally hasn't set foot in my room since we moved here.

We just sit in our silence for a minute, neither of us saying anything, while the air waits heavily for one of us to crack.

> Complex Math Problem: If two attached objects are suddenly pulled apart, the line between them now incongruent, will they ever remember how to fit together again, or is it just easier if they go their separate ways?

"What's in the box?" I finally ask.

A weary smile grows on Hannah's face. She doesn't look at me. "Christmas stuff. I found the Advent calendar."

My coldness toward Hannah melts a bit when she says that. The Advent calendar is our *thing*. Maybe fitting together isn't so hard when we're not so solidly held in our stubborn position.

The Advent calendar is a small wooden Christmas tree, and every day of Advent, leading up to Christmas, we hung one ornament on it. Hannah and I would rotate who got to hang an ornament when we were kids, which seems kind of stupid now, but it wasn't back then. It was the best. Then on Christmas morning, Mom made an angel food birthday cake for Jesus, and we sang "Happy Birthday" to him as Hannah and I together put the star on top of the Advent calendar.

We did that before Tom ever came into our lives.

"I just needed to check to make sure we had it, and that it didn't break," Hannah says. She emphasizes *needed* like she's desperate. Like she's struggling to breathe and *needs* a lifeline to the past as badly as I do.

"Did it survive the move?" I ask.

Hannah nods, and we both exhale in unison.

"Can I put a star on your ceiling?" she asks. How can I say no to that? Not with the unharmed Advent calendar right next to us. It survived, and we'll put it out in just a few weeks, and Christmas in New Mexico will have a piece of Christmas in Ohio, even if it doesn't snow.

Hannah climbs on my bed, a hesitant smile growing slowly on her face, but when she jumps, sticking a glow-in-the-dark star to my ceiling perfectly, she comes down in full glory, transformed into pure happiness. She loses her footing slightly, and I catch her before she falls off the bed. The sound of her giggle lightens the usual weight that dangles between us.

"Can I do another one?" she asks.

And all of a sudden, Hannah and I are bouncing on the bed, peppering my ceiling with so many stars I think I might actually believe I'm outside when I sleep in here. With every jump, her hair floats around her head, blocking my view until all I see is this floating orb of auburn hair that seems to radiate in the sunlight coming through the window. She and I are practically weightless. Even when our feet hit the mattress, it's only a brief landing before another lofty assent.

"Would you rather have the ability to fly or read people's minds?" Hannah asks. It's the game we played when we were little, on car trips to see our grandma in Pennsylvania.

"Fly," I say, my short hair finding buoyancy as I bounce.

"I knew that." And I actually *feel* Hannah smile. "Would you rather be blind or deaf?"

"Deaf," I say. "Totally."

"Oh my gosh, me, too." She says it with an exhale, like she is so happy we still have something in common. Maybe Hannah really did come in here to find something. Maybe she came in here to find us again. I swear I hear my bed heave a sigh of relief to have us back together. It holds her like a memory of when we were younger, when sleeping in the same bed felt like a treat, because we would stay up whispering and giggling, eventually curled around each other in the morning, our noses touching. It's been waiting for her to come back.

If Beth isn't who I thought she is, maybe the same is true for Hannah.

"Would you rather have short hair or long hair?" she asks.

My stomach turns sour at the question. I stop jumping. It's a trick. I cut my hair short after I found out I was pregnant.

Hannah asks the question again, this time with more edge to her voice.

I sit down on the end of the bed, my feet touching a box that's hidden by the bed skirt. Hannah isn't asking about my hair. She's asking about the baby. Would I erase it all and go back to being the sister I was, the girl with long hair and no secrets? Would I choose her over the baby?

Hannah takes the space next to me, but the distance between us is vast. For a moment, I thought it wasn't. What I *do* know is that Hannah and I are damaged, and it's going to take a lot more than an Advent calendar and the smell of angel food cake to put us back together. The calendar may have survived the move, but I'm not sure we did.

"Esther?" Hannah's tone is colder now. "Would you rather have short hair or long hair?"

Hannah came to see me the night the baby was born. She didn't say anything, but she stood in the doorway of my dark hospital room, outlined by the light from the hallway. I was pretending to sleep, but I peeked and saw her. I was alone, and she knew it.

She left me anyway. That night a baby cried in the room next door. I stuffed my face in a pillow and screamed.

No one heard me, because no one was there to listen.

I can't trust Hannah. I used to, but not anymore. And I won't answer her question.

I move to stand protectively in front of my fish and say, "Aren't you the one who always has the answer?"

19

Ms. Sylvia loads the choir members onto one of those church vans that fits a gazillion people and has a bumper sticker that says GOD ANSWERS KNEE-MAIL and depicts a person praying. It's headed for the Truth or Consequences Happy Day Retirement Community. Hannah is packed in that van like a sardine, alongside other choir members. I can see her through the window, squished next to Peter. She notices me looking, wraps her arm around his neck, and kisses him on the cheek. It's gross, and just another reminder that our relationship is different now.

Beth and I load heavy frozen turkeys into the back of her car. I look at the cold dead animal in my arms. Does Beth feel like a turkey in a world of chickens? How do I tell her I'm the biggest chicken of all?

"I don't even eat turkey," Beth says, loading another frozen dead animal into her trunk. "I'm a vegetarian."

Beth is wearing another doozy of a T-shirt today that says #HASHTAGSSUCK. Beth is cool enough for hashtags. She can hashtag all day long.

#imgayandproud

#andmyparentsarecoolwithit

#idontlielikeestherdoes

#becauseim*me*andfreakingrad

I want to slink into the ground and cover myself with dirt and slimy worms. Beth reveals who she is like it's as easy as pulling back a curtain and showing the world your insides. She's cracked her chest open and shown me her heart that's so beautiful I can barely stand it. And she doesn't eat meat. She's like the best person in the world, maybe next to Color. I'm such a coward. I'm still grasping at my curtain, squeezing it closed. And now, I need her to help me if I'm ever going to see Dharma today, but I can't stop stalling. At no point will this get easier, and yet I delay. Beth wouldn't do that. She's a freaking buffalo. Buffalos walk straight into a storm, whereas cows run from the impending cloud.

Moo.

The other kicker in this equation of doom is that I like Beth. She isn't who I thought she is. She's better. She's way better. And now, she might not like *me*, after *I* avoided her for over a month.

Beth slams her trunk closed and smacks her hands together like she's dusting dirt off them. "All set."

I look at the back seat. A few of the turkeys wouldn't fit in the trunk, so now Beth and I have dead passengers taking up the rear. With so much frozen stuff, the inside of the car is cold and smells like a freezer. I start to shake in the passenger seat, pretending it's just because of the turkeys.

I point at Beth's shirt, my bottom lip quivering a bit. "I like your T-shirt."

Beth rolls down her window to let warm air into the car.

"Thanks for telling me you're gay, too."

"No biggie," she says.

Ummmmm . . . Yes, biggie.

I rub my arms and give myself a small hug, all while taking a deep breath, but my body still shakes.

"Are you OK, Esther?"

I swallow a gulp of air as I look at Beth and her shirt. I could never pull off that irony. I bet Beth thinks hashtags are ridiculous. I bet she's one of those people who writes texts in perfect English. I bet she doesn't shorten words like "u" and "thx" and "LMK." I bet she writes out "Let me know" because it would be cheating the words to cut them short. That's the kind of person Beth is. She doesn't want to cheat anything. She's a vegetarian delivering frozen turkeys, because if a turkey is dead, it needs to be eaten by somebody. Beth sits in the front seat so unabashedly herself. Unashamed.

And me—I'm held together by strings. My pieces would fall apart if someone cut me in the right place.

"What's going on?" Beth sounds concerned, and I don't want her to be concerned. I want her to be my friend.

"Hashtag!" I say it like she just won the showcase showdown on *The Price Is Right*. "I had a baby!" I wave my hands out at my side, all flaring jazz fingers, my face lit up.

Beth doesn't move. I swear I can feel the weight of every cumulous cloud circling the planet at one thousand miles an hour.

Then she says, "Hashtag—holy shit."

∞

"Have you ever done this before?" Amit asked, eyes wide as he sat on my bed. Mom was at Zumba. Hannah was at ballet. I was at a turning point.

"No," I said. "You?"

"No," Amit said with a slight chuckle. He rubbed the spot on his head where his hair refused to lie flat. "You were the first girl I ever even kissed."

"Should I close my eyes?"

"Why?"

"People on TV always close their eyes. Maybe it makes it easier."

"No," he said, his hand moving from his hair to my cheek. He was shaking. It only made me more certain that what I was about to do was right. When people stand on the edge of change, ready to jump, they should be nervous. But we were standing together. "I need to look at you, Esther. Eyes open."

"OK," I said, cupping Amit's hand with mine. "Eyes open."

∞

"Open your eyes, Esther . . . Open your eyes."

I know I should follow the command, but I'm too scared to look at the present right now; I'd rather drift warmly off into the cozy past for just a moment longer.

"Seriously, open your eyes." Beth's demand is forceful, but her voice carries kindness even through the cold filling the car.

I peek at her with one eye.

"Whoa," Beth says.

"Yeah," I say. "That's why I need to go see Dharma." I tell her everything, spilling my guts, and then I apologize for the mess. I am a messy person. No matter where I go, I spill.

"Whoa," Beth says again. She's staring straight ahead, like she's driving, but we're still sitting in the church parking lot.

I look out the window at Touchdown Jesus and say to him silently, *If Hannah is right and you're all about love, you better not take Beth away from me.* And then I feel guilty because it's not Jesus's fault. He gets blamed for enough. This is my fault.

"You gave up the baby for adoption?" Beth asks.

I nod.

"But you never got to see her or hold her?"

I shake my head, my arms feeling weighted and empty at the same time. My words are failing me.

"And you're worried you made the wrong decision?"

Beth's question gives me pause, like all her other questions. I shouldn't be surprised, but this one has me slightly stunned. The wrong decision? I'm not sure I made the wrong decision so much as I made *no* decision. I didn't have a hand in the answer. It was just given to me. I want to come to my own conclusion. I want to solve the problem for myself. *That's* what I feel I was robbed of. That's what I feel I need to find. I tell Beth exactly that.

"Whoa."

Beth's eyes get big, and then small, as she mumbles to herself. The longer she stays quiet, the more fear starts to take over any hope that Beth would understand. The air in the vehicle that weighs one hundred pounds is now also filled with my baggage. And all Beth has to do is open the door to let it spill all over the church parking lot, and it's all over for me.

"Please don't tell anyone," I say.

Beth looks at me with bulging eyes. "Why would I do that?"

"Because I didn't tell you sooner. Because I'm a liar and a former pregnant teen whose family made her move across the country to get away from the shame of it all. I should probably have my own MTV show. And because you're *so* you, and I'm confused as to who I am. Because you can pull off a hashtag shirt even though I know you hate hashtags."

Beth grins. "You get the irony."

"That's another thing. I'm not one hundred percent sure how to use irony. People seem to mess that up a lot. I'd probably use it all wrong."

Then Beth laughs and leans across the seat, wrapping her arms around my neck.

"Going to see a psychic is so much better than delivering turkeys," Beth says. She pulls back, and because things like this are effortless for Beth, I see the truth all over her face. Beth smiles and the sun shines.

"I hope you don't mind," I say, "but we have a few more turkeys we need to pick up first."

20

It turns that out Beth is in a lot of the same classes as Jesús, even though she's a junior and he's a senior. She's just that smart. And she's seen him at HuggaMug. Beth drinks coffee, too. I should have known. Color is just so excited that the universe is constantly putting pieces of the puzzle together, and we all fit so well. And I have to admit, I get a little jealous that they all go to school together, while the only person in my class is Hannah.

Jesús looks into the back of Beth's car at all the frozen turkeys and says, "That's a lot of turkeys."

"We need to deliver them at some point," Beth says. "Or we'll get busted."

We decide to unload the frozen turkeys into the garage, to be dropped off after we get back from Albuquerque.

Halfway through the process, Moss comes outside and says, "What's going on?"

"We're going to Albuquerque to find the truth," Color says.

Jesús holds up his notebook. "I'm prepared to document the findings."

"Why didn't you tell me?" Moss says. "I want to come."

And I almost faint. He *never* wants to do anything with us.

We're on the road headed north out of Truth or Consequences so soon after that it almost feels surreal. Beth drives, and Color sits next to her. I'm sandwiched in the back between Jesús and Moss, and every few minutes, Moss's leg touches my leg and he pulls away. Like I'm untouchable. Moss is like irony. I'm not really sure how he works.

I tell them about the "Would You Rather" game Hannah and I played on car trips, and Jesús totally geeks out.

"Would you rather swim through shit or dead bodies?" he asks.

"Neither," Moss says. "I choose death."

"That's cheating." Jesús leans over and slaps Moss's leg with the red licorice he's eating. "Esther, tell Fungus he's cheating. You have to pick."

"You have to pick," I say. "That's how the game is played."

Jesús offers me some licorice, but I'm too nervous to eat. He leans across me to hand some to Moss and inadvertently forces my leg into Moss's. Moss can't pull away this time because we're squashed.

"Fine," Moss says, snapping a piece of licorice in his mouth. "Shit. I pick the shit."

"Me, too," Jesús says. He sits back in his seat, rolls down the window, and sticks his head out so his brown hair blows in the wind.

And this time Moss doesn't move his leg.

"Me, three," Color says.

"Me, four," I add.

"Me, five," Beth says from the front seat.

One. Two. Three. Four. Five. How did this happen? I'm not sure I want to know the answer. I just want to feel good right now. I just want to feel like I'm not alone. I don't want to worry how it all occurred or how it might all fall apart. The lies I'm feeding my family seem to be stacking up like the turkeys in Color's garage, but if they stay hidden and stacked, I can keep them.

Beth's necklace dangles on the outside of her shirt, and I take a risk, deciding to talk to the Big Guy again, since she seems to get along with him.

God, please don't take my friends away. Also, why do people always assume you're a man? Are you really a woman, like Beth is really gay, but you haven't said anything because people are idiots? If that's the case, it's a smart move. Nice going, God. Now, I know why you and Beth get along so well.

"My turn." Color turns around in her seat. "Would you rather eat shit that tastes like chocolate or eat chocolate that tastes like shit?"

Moss argues that even if you eat chocolate that tastes like shit, you're still eating chocolate, so you can at least feel good about that. But Jesús counters with the fact that if the shit tastes like chocolate, you'd forget that it's shit. Beth says she's with Moss. She'd take the chocolate flat out, and I like her even more.

When we pull into Albuquerque, the car goes quiet for a while. The only person talking is the woman telling us directions from Beth's phone. She speaks in an English accent.

"Turn right in five hundred feet," she says properly.

Jesús rests his head back on the seat. "Everything sounds better in a British accent."

"Totally." Color perfectly mimics the voice coming from the phone. We all smile.

But as the buildings become denser and we're surrounded by more cars, it hits me that we really aren't in Truth or Consequences anymore. A sense of utter fear makes my whole body tingle.

"Maybe this was a bad idea," I say. I have a carload of people who I've dragged on this trip, and what if Dharma doesn't give me any answers? Or worse, what if I don't like what I hear? "Let's turn around. I've changed my mind."

But Color looks back at me. "You can't turn around, love. That's not how time works." She's doing the British accent again. "Your only choice is to move forward."

Color really is a genius. Jesús puts his hand on my thigh. Moss's leg still touches mine, and there's no way he doesn't know it. Beth looks at me hopefully in the rearview mirror, and I think British accents really do make everything better.

∞

"You're here for answers," Dharma says.

"Oh my God, it's already working." Jesús gawks.

"Color told me over the phone when we talked." Dharma looks at Color. "Please tell your mom I say hello. She and I have traveled through many lives. Some even together."

"I will," Color says, and then adds under her breath, "next time I see her. Whenever that is."

From the outside of Dharma's house, you'd never know a psychic lives here. It's a traditional adobe home, all sand and more sand, except for the windows, doors, and roof fixtures that are painted a baby blue.

Inside it smells like rich incense. Colorful curtains decorate the windows, where multiple crystals are lined up on the sill. New Age chiming music plays in the background. Tom would kill me if he knew I was here. Like complete murder in the first. He wouldn't even bother burying the body. I glance at Beth to make sure she's not absolutely freaking out her Science-Christian mind, but she looks totally enthralled.

She points at a pink crystal. "Rose quartz?" she asks Dharma.

"Heals the negative energy in the heart," Dharma says.

Jesús picks up the crystal and holds it to Moss's chest. "Tell me when it starts working."

Moss pushes his hand away, his cheeks getting red. "Shut up."

Jesús hands the rose quartz to Dharma. "This thing is clearly broken."

Dharma laughs and touches Moss with compassion. "Just like your dad."

"You know my dad?" he asks, with more enthusiasm in his voice than I've ever heard.

Dharma takes his hand. "I know a lot of things. That doesn't mean I understand them."

This is getting weird.

She gestures toward the large couch in her living room. We move in a pack, Dharma following behind us. When we all sit down on the couch, it sighs under our weight.

Dharma settles in an oversized leather chair that's worn to her body and fits her perfectly. I wish I had a chair like that.

"You're here for answers, which must mean you have some questions."

That's an understatement, I think. Dharma smiles in a way that tells me she just heard me talking to myself. Holy crap.

"Yes," Color says. "Esther needs answers."

"She's not the only one." Dharma looks at my friends with a knowing eye.

"So far you are earning your money," Jesús says. He folds his hands over his knees.

"I have to warn you—answers can be overrated. Some people don't want to hear what I have to say. Are you sure you *want* to do this?"

My friends look at me. Want? Need? I'm drowning in an empty pool that Tom refuses to fill with water. Am I sure I want to do this? No. But am I sure I've made the right decisions? No. From where I'm sitting, I don't have a choice. With a nod, I tell Dharma to continue.

She sits forward in her seat, closing the space between us. "I must inform you that I can only tell you what I see. I can't tell you how to interpret it."

"OK," I say.

Dharma says, "Now, give me your hand."

That I can do. I place my hand in hers. Her skin is kind of cold, but against my hot hand, it feels nice. Dharma traces the lines of my palm with her finger. She touches the calluses from my handlebars.

Then she looks at me. "Wow. You've been through a lot."

"Seriously, you're amazing," Jesús says.

Color nudges him and whispers, "Shhh."

Dharma's eyes don't shift from mine. "And it's not over."

"It's not?" I say.

"No." Dharma shakes her head. "The journey is never over, my dear."

"Well, what am I supposed to do? Which way am I supposed to go?" I ask more ardently.

Dharma shakes her head. "I told you—I can't tell you that." Her eyes focus down at my palm again. "But I can tell you that souls have mates. That we do not travel into this life alone. We are connected to people by something that is beyond our human knowing. But the ever-present Soul knows." Dharma places my hand and her hand on top of my heart. "The Soul feels beyond this world."

"That's what my mom says!" Color pipes up.

Now it's Jesús's turn to say, "Shhhh!" He leans forward in his seat.

"That's what this journey is about," Dharma adds.

I shake my head and feel tears sting my eyes. "But what do I do?"

There's a long, gut-wrenching pause as Dharma stares at the wall behind us, like she's checked out of the session. She's gone vacant. This is truly horrible timing. I need her to focus. The moment I'm about to snap my fingers in front of her face, anger pulsing low in my belly, she takes both our hands away from my heart, her hand falling limp to her lap. I don't know what to do. Is that it? Did we come all the way to Albuquerque for her to give me the same answer I already know? That I'm missing a piece. That answers just lead to more questions. She hasn't solved anything.

"Where do I go from here?" I beg.

Dharma inhales deeply. Beth, Color, Moss, and Jesús look at me totally confused. Join the damn freaking psychic club! While we're in Albuquerque, turkeys are melting in Truth or Consequences. We need to get home. Every second we're here, I can feel myself getting closer to total destruction. With a jolt, Dharma grabs my hand again and brings it to her nose.

"Water," Dharma says suddenly, still gazing off at God knows what. Literally, God only knows what. "You're covered in water, Esther." She sniffs my hand deeply again. "And . . ."

"What?" I beg.

More sniffing. "Salt. I smell salt."

"Salt water? But we're in the desert," Jesús says. "The ocean is, like, a million miles away."

Dharma and I link, like she's in my brain and I'm in hers. The feeling that all people in the world are connected—every single one of us, by the skin that covers our bodies and the hearts that pump our blood and the love we wish we had—consumes me.

"This journey you're on," she says. "It ends at the ocean. There you will find what you're looking for. But I think you already knew this, Esther."

"The ocean?" Color says. "What's at the ocean?"

Dharma lets go of my hand as I sit back on the couch. My entire body hums.

"The baby," I whisper. "She's in California."

Jesús gasps. "It worked! She had the answer." He gets out his notebook and a pen. "Dharma, I have this senior project I need to complete. Can you tell me what my truth is?"

21

Complex Math Problem: The square mileage of California is one of the highest in the country, which begs the question—Is it possible to find a needle in a haystack?

We have to save the turkeys. They're sitting in Color's garage defrosting. After our quick goodbyes, no one says anything for a long time as we drive, because what is there to say?

Once we're miles outside of Albuquerque, the city barely a speck in the distance, Beth finally says, "You're absolutely sure the baby went to a family in California?"

"Yes," I say.

"Do you know where?" she asks.

I shake my head. "That's all my mom would tell me."

"California is a big state," Moss offers.

I glare at him. He can take his offering and shove it up his ass.

"Sorry." He sounds like he means it.

"But now we know what we have to do." Color hasn't lost her enthusiasm. For everything she's been through in life—no dad, a mom who comes and goes on a whim, a brother who's about as expressive as the moss that shares his name—she stays bright. "We need to go to California. Duh."

"Yes!" Jesús echoes.

"I'm in," Beth says without hesitation.

"I've never seen the ocean before," Moss say. "I'd like that."

Right. Duh. California. It took multiple lies just to get us to Albuquerque, a two-hour drive. A day trip. California is, like, at least a three-day trip. It may actually be a new-life trip, because I will be dead if Mom or Tom ever figure out I went there. To see the baby. A baby produced by having sex with a boy. Now we're talking about running off to California. My life in New Mexico is not moving in the direction Tom had hoped. Turns out, there are problems everywhere. Problems are infinite.

"Sometimes the best answer we get is infinity," Amit said once. "No matter how many times we rework the problem."

Infinity is air through your fingers when all you want is a solid object.

Seeing Dharma today hasn't solved anything. It's only complicated my life.

It will take too many lies to get to California. Why do I always have to lie? Why can't I be like Beth and Color and Jesús? Just say what I want and who I am and not have the world turn upside down.

"No," I say. "No California."

"But what about everything Dharma said?" Color counters. "Your journey. It ends at the ocean."

"Maybe she's wrong," I say. "I don't even know where to start."

Beth says, "Well—"

But I cut her off, because my blood is pumping so hard, and my heart is heavy. I can't keep lying and hurting people.

"No," I say more emphatically. "No California. It's over."

I press my hand to my nose. It just smells like a hand. I can't smell salt like Dharma could. And we're over one thousand miles from California. But I knew that before. Now all I know is that it's *really* out of reach. California feels farther than ever. I may know now that it's where I need to go, but getting there hasn't become any easier.

I want to scream. Why does it have to be so hard? Why do I constantly keep running into the same wall? That's what crazy people do. They repeat the same action, expecting a different result. I love math, for Christ's sake! I know one plus one equals two, and yet I keep hoping it will equal three.

I bow my head, and Jesús puts his hand on my knee.

"The truth sucks," he says.

"Just think about it, Esther," Color says. "You might change your mind."

With all the effort I have left, I shake my head and then rest it heavily back on the seat.

Moss rolls his hands together next to me. His legs bounce like he's anxious. He's holding the rose quartz from Dharma.

When he notices me staring at it, he says, "She gave it to me."

I wish what she gave me was that concrete. Moss's legs just keep bouncing.

"Would you stop that?" I bark at him, and then instantly feel bad. I'm not the only person missing things. Color and Moss are missing a dad. Beth is missing her first love. And Jesús . . . I watch him as he lets the wind coming in the car cover him, his eyes a piece of the sun. He's missing his truth.

"I'm sorry. I'm antsy. I need to go for a run," Moss whispers. "You can come with me if you want."

"Can't," I say. "Turkeys."

It isn't until we pull into Color's driveway that anyone speaks again, Color talking first.

"Sweet Jesus," she says.

Jesús is resting his head back on the seat with his eyes closed. "It's pronounced Hey-soos."

"No." Color points to her driveway.

"Sweet Jesus," Moss echoes, his face painted in awe.

"What is it?" I sit up straighter to see through the windshield. There's a car in the driveway that I don't recognize and a woman standing in the garage looking at all the frozen turkeys. My first thought is that we're busted.

"Color, start talking in that British accent again and make this better," Moss says.

The woman standing in the driveway has long black hair knotted into dreadlocks that hang clear down her back. Her jeans are ripped, and her white T-shirt hangs off one shoulder, exposing her thin frame.

Color's face is broken into pieces of happiness and pieces of dread. They fit together to make a collage of emotion and color.

In her perfect British accent, she says, "It's our mum."

22

I'm starting to think that maybe loving someone means lying to them. Mom found Tom on a Christian dating website back when we only went to church on Christmas and Easter, but Mom said our religious status was good enough, and Tom didn't need to know all the details. She was lying.

I asked Amit not to tell anyone about the baby, and he did it for me. For love. Amit has been lying ever since.

Color looks at Moss and says, "Would you rather have a mom who was home all the time or a mom who's barely ever home?"

Moss stares ahead and says, "You know the answer."

And Color says, "Me, too."

And for just a second, the car holds us together.

"I'm sorry I snapped at you," I whisper to Moss.

"That's OK. I deserved it."

"Esther, can you tell us a joke?" Color says.

"Why was the obtuse triangle always upset?"

"Why?" Color says.

"Because it was never right."

Color laughs. So does Moss. And then suddenly Color and Moss are running down the driveway to lovingly hug their mom, who left them to scam money off their grandma in Denver, and Beth, Jesús, and I are left to marinate in the truth.

Love is lying.

And we need to be back at church in less than two hours. The turkeys are defrosting.

Jesús offers to help with the delivery. We leave Color and Moss standing in the driveway, dressed in lies that make people feel better.

We barely make it back to church on time. Jesús tells Beth just to drop him at HuggaMug to save time. He'll get home just fine.

Pastor Rick stands in front of the church. I ask Beth why she doesn't trust him.

"He's too perfect," she says. "Everyone has flaws. He works too hard to hide his."

> Complex Math Problem: If love is lying, does that
> mean that if I stop lying, I'll never love again?

At home, I decide to go through the boxes of clothes in my closet. I finally need to let go of some things from my past. I need to be honest with myself. I will no longer hold on to anything that shouldn't be held on to. Or at least, I'll try.

∞

Jesús works by himself on Thanksgiving, because people don't take holidays from coffee, and Moss is spending the day with his mom. My mom suggests I get out for a bike ride before we spend the rest of the day eating, and I promptly ride to HuggaMug to see Jesús and to get an iced soy mocha frap. My lies are the only weight I intend to lose.

I bring Jesús an old apron I found in one of the boxes. My aunt Emily made Hannah and me matching ones for Christmas a few years ago. The edge is lined with white eyelets. Jesús loves it. He spins in a circle, modeling it as I sit on the couch inside the hut.

"For life's many messes," I say.

"Are you sure you don't want it, mon chéri?" Jesús washes metal containers in the sink.

"An apron isn't going to help my messes."

His back is to me. "Are you still thinking about California?"

Always. Infinitely. Yes. Double yes. Those are my answers. I nod when he turns around.

Jesús wipes his hands on the apron. "Why don't we go?"

My nodding becomes shaking. "I promised myself I'd stop lying."

"How's that going?"

"Well, I'm here with you instead of riding my bike, so not that well." I put a finger in the air. "But from this moment on, I am not going to lie anymore. At least, not about things that matter."

"Well, I'm not sure this apron is going to help with my messes, either, but at least I look good." Jesús sits next to me and leans his head on my shoulder. "Can I ask you something? Since you're not lying anymore. And this matters."

"Sure."

"Does God hate me?"

I sit back, completely surprised.

Jesús plays with the eyelet trimming on the apron. "You know God better than I do. You go to church and all."

"I don't know. He's kind of given me the silent treatment ever since I committed a pretty big sin." It's Hannah who carries around a Bible, Hannah who loves going to church and singing in the choir and ogling over Pastor Rick, because he's just *awesome*.

"It's just . . . Why did he make some people gay?" Jesús asks. "Why couldn't he just make me . . . normal?"

"What's normal?" I ask.

"You know—penises that want to go into vaginas. It's not that I would turn down a vagina but . . ." Jesús picks up the frothing wand. "I really want a penis." And then he adds, "Other than mine."

The frothing wand is covered in milk. Jesús licks it. I toss a couch pillow at him. He catches it and hugs it to his chest.

"Seriously, mon chéri, be honest—*Does* God hate me? It really seems like he does sometimes."

Honestly, honesty is really overrated.

"First of all . . ." I take the pillow from Jesús. "You assume God is a man. God could be a unicorn."

"A unicorn God would never hate gays." Jesús puts his head back on my shoulder.

"OK, honestly?" I say.

"Yes," Jesús says. "Honestly."

"I don't have the answer."

He exhales, like that was what he expected. I know that disappointment.

"Since we've decided to be truthful right now, can I tell you something?" Jesús says.

"Sure," I whisper into his hair.

"I think you're crazy not to go to California. And I know you have a million questions and a million excuses, but she's your kid, and you should at least *see* her."

"There are *reasons* I can't go."

"No, mon chéri—they're excuses. Take it from me. Love isn't abundant. If there were people out in the world who could love me, and they had a way of finding me, I'd want them to do it."

Jesús and I sink into the couch and exhale together.

"Make sure to write that down as research for your senior statement," I say.

"Which part?"

"Love isn't abundant."

"Damn . . ." Jesús says. "This telling the truth stuff is really overrated."

The bell rings, announcing that a car has pulled up, and Jesús jumps to action. I need to get home soon. Mom will want help mashing the potatoes.

"Welcome to HuggaMug; let me help you today," Jesús says out the window. He glances back at me and winks. I gesture toward the bathroom.

I pee quickly and wash my hands, but can't find any towels. I search the cabinet under the sink, but no luck in the paper-towel department. I do find a Dopp kit filled with shaving cream, toothpaste, a toothbrush, and hair gel. That's odd. I pick up the shaving cream.

Maybe it's where Moss shaves his head, which is super gross.

When I come out of the bathroom with wet hands, Jesús offers me his apron to dry them. He's always helping other people.

"Is your family doing anything fun for Thanksgiving?" I ask.

But the bell dings and another car pulls up. Jesús says, "Welcome to HuggaMug; let me help you today."

∞

Hannah's Bible is on the coffee table. I lean against the wall, gnawing on my lip.

"You're pregnant?" Hannah's younger voice echoes in my ears. I imagine her sitting on the love seat that occupies our spacious living room in New Mexico. It looks small for the room here, but in Ohio we had less space, and a love seat nestled perfectly into our lives.

As I sit on the too-small couch, my memory of Hannah in eighth grade settles in next to me.

She found out I was pregnant when she overheard an eighth-grade teacher gossiping about it with another teacher. That's the kind of town we lived in—words moved quicker than wind and destroyed things faster than tornadoes.

"You've had sex?" she said. "With who?"

"It's none of your business."

"You're not going to tell me? But you always promised you'd tell me everything," she said, her voice weak.

"Well, I lied," I said. Remembering that makes me want to throw up.

"How could you not tell me?" Hannah trailed off, broken into pieces. "You promised . . ."

"Just leave me alone."

I muster the courage to look at the space next to me on the love seat, but no one is there. Hannah's Bible rests on the table, some sort of symbol of our blocked relationship. Hannah uses it as a shield, a way to defend herself against me. To push me away. Is that why it was written in the first place? To keep the outsiders out and the believers in? But if no one else is telling the truth, why should I believe what's in there, anyway? If love is lying, then maybe what's written in the Bible is just one big lie, masquerading as love.

"What are you doing?" Hannah's voice is now deeper, and serious. An older, tanner version of my sister shows herself, her cantaloupe chest puffed out proudly. The Hannah I had just remembered felt uncomfortable about her large breasts and wore sports bras to squash them down. Not anymore. I don't know if it's the clothes that hug her body in all the right places, or her straight posture, or the fact that she *is* growing older and further away from me, but the distance between us feels nearly infinite. I nonchalantly sit back on the love seat, knowing she won't sit next to me, and watching her as she watches me, skeptically.

I caught her and Peter holding hands in choir. Like, the whole practice. Maybe *caught* isn't the right word so much as *noticed*, like everyone else did. It was pretty obvious.

She grabs the Bible and hugs it to herself. "Did you look at this?"

"No," I say, annoyed that she's annoyed. What if I had? That's the question I want to spit at Hannah. What's so wrong with me looking at her precious book?

"Good."

Hannah moves to leave, but I say, "What's going on with you and Peter?"

She whips around. "*Now*, you want to be girlfriends? You want me to tell you all my secrets? Pardon me as I laugh." And then she does that condescending fake laugh thing, and I regret asking.

"Forget it." I need to get out of here.

Hannah's older voice, a reminder that time never moves backward, trails after me, down the hallway, as I disappear into my room. "Just remember, Esther—who walked away first?"

Because Hannah follows orders, she listened to me all those months ago when I told her to leave me alone. I guess I shouldn't be mad it's lasted this long. I asked for it.

23

Color pushes the vacuum back and forth in my room, robotically. The spark that twinkles in her eyes most days is dim today. If I could take all the stars from my ceiling and give that light back to her, I would. I try to wait patiently for her to talk. When she's vacuumed the same strip of carpet ten times, Color finally says, "My mom's selling the Blockbuster. That's why she's home."

"What?" I say too harshly.

Color struggles to hold back tears. "We need the money, and she was only holding on to the Blockbuster for me." She stops vacuuming. "It's like the end of an era, and I knew it couldn't last because nothing lasts—that's the nature of life—but the Blockbuster is Heaven, so I just thought maybe it would be different this time."

Color tells me they cooked one of the frozen turkeys for Thanksgiving, and that the house was so filled with love and good smells that it really felt like a holiday. That's when her mom dropped the Blockbuster bomb.

Color imitates a bomb dropping and hissing and exploding on my floor. And then she flops over on my bed, like she's so exhausted she just can't stand anymore. Color's grandma doesn't have as much money as Color's mom thought, and bills are bills, and they need to be paid. On time, preferably.

"I know I shouldn't be disappointed," Color says. "I know we need to do this to, like, keep our house and stuff. But it's like Heaven is dying. And I would never tell my mom how much it hurts because I love her, but it hurts a little."

"I'm sorry," I say.

Color puts her head in her hands. "What am I going to do with everything I've saved? I can't just get rid of it."

I wish I could make it better. I wish I could force Color's mom to make better decisions. I wish love wasn't so complicated.

Color points to the windowsill where my fish is. "At least we still have the fish. Did you figure out a name yet?"

I shake my head.

"Well, it will come to you. And you put the stars on your ceiling." My galaxy twinkles over Color's head. "So many suns that only come out to light the darkness. It's so poetic."

I lie down next to her so our heads touch. If I stay here long enough, can I get Color's knowledge through osmosis? Because that would be poetic.

"Beth told me that the sun will burn out in five billion years," I say.

"Beth is so freaking awesome."

"It's crazy that one day it won't exist."

"Nothing is permanent," Color says. "I'm really feeling that truth right now."

"Except infinity," I say. "It goes on and on and on and on and on and on and on . . ."

Color rolls onto her side. "I like when you speak Math."

As we lie together, wrapped in sad smiles, I feel the moment passing, carried out the window and into infinity. Someday it will reach the sun and beyond.

Eventually Color says, "Am I destined to be just like my mom? You know, the whole 'Cat's in the Cradle' thing. Ending up like her is just . . . inevitable. Is that my 'truth statement'?"

"Nothing is inevitable," I say.

I think I see relief cross Color's face. "Except infinity."

"Except that."

Standing up on the bed, I jump and grab for one of the stars. Color watches me, intrigued, as I place it on her forehead.

"You are your own unique star," I say. "And I've made a vow to only tell the truth, so you can believe me when I say that."

"Only telling the truth? What's the fun in that?" Color laughs, touching the star between her eyebrows. "It's on my third eye." When my total confusion registers, she says, "Your sixth chakra. The seat of intuition."

She imitates meditating, sitting up straight and closing her eyes softly, her palms open and facing up on her thighs.

"You're speaking in Dharma language now," I say. "I have no idea what you're talking about."

Color touches the star, her eyes still shut. "It's like your gut, but in your head. It's like that thing that tells you, 'This is your path, Esther Ainsworth, now follow it.' My mom says it's meant to guide you, if you let it."

Her moment of meditation complete, Color jumps and grabs another star. She puts it on my forehead, the third eye that I was unaware of until this very moment, though it's been with me the entire time. Color leaves her hand pressed to my forehead, closing her eyes again as if she's trying to read my thoughts.

"What's your intuition telling you?" I ask.

She opens one eye. "My intuition is telling me that we knew each other in a past life. It's also telling me that you're eating chili for dinner." And then she freezes and sucks in a breath. "And . . . oh my God."

"What?"

"Oh my God. It worked." She starts jumping on the bed. And because she's jumping, I start to jump, too, even though I'm not sure what we're jumping about. But suddenly, it feels like I'm on my old trampoline again, the rusty springs giving way but ultimately catching us again and again.

"What is it?" I ask.

"Infinity! Reincarnation! That's the answer!" Color is so ecstatic that I can barely keep up with her jumping.

"What?"

"I don't have to get rid of everything in Heaven!" Color jumps and jumps and jumps. "I need to give it brand new life!"

"How?" My sight is blurring with all our movement. All I can see is the star marking Color's forehead. Her intuition floats through the air, glowing, and I wonder if mine is doing the same.

"We'll hold a garage sale for all the lost items in Heaven," Color says. "They can finally be reborn!" She gets off the bed, her feet returning to solid ground, the light back in her eyes. "We'll give everything a brand new life."

∞

It turns out Color was right—Mom does cook chili for dinner. Also, my intuition is so freaking broken. I want a new one. The empty pool surrounds me as I lie on the cracked floor, a glow-in-the-dark star on my third eye, waiting for my intuition to show up. It's drifting and mingling with the suns above.

I ask, *Are you there?*

I ask, *Can you hear me?*

I ask, *Do you speak a different language? Because I'm having a hard time hearing you.*

I ask, *Just tell me this—Is the ocean warm in California?*

I ask, *Do you think Tom will ever fill this pool?*

Nothing. Nothing. Nothing.

I ask, *Did I have an intuition to begin with?*

That's what Tom said was the worst part of all. That I didn't think having sex with Amit was wrong.

Tom: *Sex* out of wedlock is a *sin*.

Tom: *Sex* is *sacred*.

Tom: *Sex* is *something* you *save* for *someday* when you meet *someone special*.

He kept exaggerating all the *S*s and I wanted to scream, *Just say it like a normal person instead of the snake tattooed on your arm, you lunatic!*

He never said what I felt, which was that sex is love. I guess there weren't enough *S*s.

Maybe that's been my problem all along. I was born without an intuition. After all, my father left my mom with two young kids and no money. He clearly didn't have it either. Maybe it's a genetic disorder.

Hannah pokes her head out the sliding screen door and shouts, "Tom says you need to get out of that pool and come in for dinner, Esther."

I lazily sit up.

"Why do you have a star on your forehead?"

The lights coming from the house surround Hannah in a halo of yellow gold. Her breasts seem more pronounced than usual, and her hair more buoyant than ever. She is literally wearing her body like a different person, but one small move and the radiance that surrounds her would disappear.

And then I feel it. My intuition decides to pop up. There it is. Tom has a snake tattoo on his arm that he hides every day. In essence, he's lying, trying to cover up his past. Mom is lying about who I'm hanging out with, and who knows what else. Even Color is lying to her mom, in a way, by not telling her how much it hurts that she's selling the Blockbuster.

And Hannah . . . I stare at her standing in the doorway, her body looking almost like a costume.

"What?" she barks at me.

129

My intuition says Hannah is lying about something, too. I'm not sure what, but I *am* sure that everyone hides something. I'm not the only one. Even the stars hide during the day. And hiding isn't necessarily lying, but liars hide the truth.

"What?" Hannah says again.

That's a good question. *What, Hannah? What are you lying about?* I ask silently.

"Take that star off your forehead," she says. "You are *so* weird." As she turns, Hannah flips her hair over her shoulder.

We may not look or sound alike, but Hannah and I are more similar than she thinks.

Liar, liar, pants on fire.

24

Complex Math Problem: If the whole world is lying,
does truth really exist?

A heat wave hits in December. *December.* This is the time of year when
it's supposed to cool down, just as Tom promised, but it's hot and dry.
The lie gets added to the pile, and I start to flake and crack.

The heat makes napping by the river hard. I'm just so darn hot,
and no one likes to sleep in sweat. That's gross. I end up sitting under
one of the small trees, trying to squeeze into as much shade as possible.

Shade in the desert is as abundant as truth is in this world of liars.

I come home every day sweating profusely, so Mom thinks I'm
really working hard at losing weight. Mom's even lying to herself.

A few months ago, I came to the river to sleep and escape, but if
I'm being honest with myself, and I'm really trying to, my reasons for
occupying my small space of shade down by the river have changed.

At the familiar pitter-patter of Moss's feet on the path, I jump out
from my patch of beautiful, cooling shade and bolt into the sunlight.
Doing this also happens to scare the crap out of Moss *again*, and I think
for a second he might pass out from fear. My track record with him is
abysmal.

Moss bends over, heaving. "I told you to stop doing that!"

"I'm sorry," I say, my eyes burning with sudden light, as Moss tries to regain his breath.

Droplets of sweat rain down from his chin to his chest. I watch them trail his body. Jealousy edges into my stomach. Has a girl made that same trek with her hands? If she has, why did Moss let her in, and not me? Has Moss allowed that access to a lot of girls? The questions only make me want to demand contact.

"I just wanted to make sure you really don't like surprises." I try to laugh off my poor choice in approaching him, but Moss only glares at me. "Sorry," I say, defeat inching closer. When I nervously kick a rock with my shoe, it hits Moss in the shin.

"Seriously?" He gapes at me.

I throw my hands up. "Forget it! I never do anything right with you!"

Hastily grabbing my bike from the ground, intent on getting the hell out of here as Moss rubs his shin, I say, "I just thought we could ride or run or whatever together. I wasn't going to talk to you or anything. But forget it."

But then Moss says, "Wait."

And I do as he says, coming to look at him hesitantly, forcing myself to be the silent one for once.

"Are you *trying* to do things right?" Moss says.

I pinch my lips closed, not wanting to offer words in case they stifle his.

"You don't need to try, Esther. You're fine just the way you are."

His words attempt to knock me over. It's what I've wanted to hear, but actually having them materialize in the air . . . I start to melt on the pavement, and not a bit of it is from the heat. Waiting in the shade for this moment in the bright sun was so worth it. With a single declaration, I'm back on the roller coaster ride, flipping around and around. But that's how powerful statements can be. They can change your life, turn it upside down, in a matter of a few words.

"You think I'm fine?" I ask Moss. Out loud.

He nods, simultaneously wiping sweat from his forehead. Today, he's wearing little running shorts that show the majority of his really muscular thighs and a sleeveless shirt. Right now, I'm wearing a blush. I can feel it heat my cheeks.

"I didn't know that you felt that way about me."

"I might not be big on talking, but that doesn't mean I don't think about things," Moss says.

"You think about . . . things . . . *me* being a thing?"

Instead of watching me, Moss examines the sweat that drips from his chin onto the hot pavement. "I think . . . I'm done running for the day."

"Oh. OK." Weren't we just having a deep conversation about *things*?

"Do you want to go for a swim?" he asks.

"Um . . . no."

Moss decides to look at me then, and my heart skips a beat. "Why not?"

"Well, for starters, I don't have a suit," I say. "And for seconds, even if I did, I wouldn't put it on."

"We can wear our clothes . . . if that will make you more comfortable." Moss is implying that we could go naked.

I picture me on a roller coaster, hands up: *Ahhhhhhh!!*

"Come on," he says. "It'll be fun."

"You have fun?" I ask with false snark. Moss pretends to be insulted, which is actually a really cute way of flirting with me. I gave that look to Amit once, pretending I was going to walk away only because I hoped he'd grab my arm and make me stop. I wanted Amit to touch me and hold me still. He did what I wanted and so much more. But that memory doesn't belong here. I cast it off into the river and let the current carry my past away.

"You know how to swim, right?" Moss walks to the river's edge, leaving me on the path.

"Of course I know how to swim," I say, more to myself than to him, as I follow him down to the water.

We stand at the edge, the river shimmering in the sunlight. With no wind, the top is as smooth as glass. I see my reflection in the blue water next to Moss.

"Do you think everyone has an intuition?" I ask.

"You've been talking to Color too much."

"I mean it. Do you think there's something greater out there?"

"My intuition is telling me that out there"—Moss points toward the center of the river—"we'll be a lot cooler than if we keep standing right here."

Moss runs into the water and disappears underneath it. When his buzzed head pops up, a wide grin brightens his face. "Come on! What are you afraid of?" He tries to splash me on the dirt.

Good question. What *am* I afraid of? Let me make a list: *Spiders, peacocks, gagging, people in masks, bananas, balloons, balloons shaped like bananas . . .*

I take off my shoes and socks and put my feet in the water.

Mannequins, Big Bird, porcelain dolls with creepy nonmoving eyes . . .

When the water is up to my knees, my profuse sweating stops. Damn, it feels good.

Moths, loose teeth that dangle by a string of my gum, rodents of unusual size . . .

The water is at wrist level now, and I skim my hands over the top, making small ripples.

That I'm damaged; that no one will ever love me again; that the world is one big lying, sucking vampire; that I'll end up alone . . .

I wade out to where Moss is treading water.

I'm afraid of letting go . . .

"See, that wasn't so hard," he says.

He doesn't know about the trail of fears I left behind.

"What are *you* afraid of?" I ask him as my arms and legs move through the water to keep me afloat.

"That I'll be stuck here forever."

He says it just like that. No hesitation. Just the truth. Moss's honesty is so surprising, I stop treading for a moment and sink in the water. I have to pull hard to get level on the surface.

"And the red tacks on the map in your room?" I ask.

"The places I want to go." And then Moss corrects himself. "The places I *need* to go."

The Rio Grande might be filled with truth serum.

"If you could go anywhere in the world, where would you go?" I ask.

"Anywhere."

"Yeah, anywhere."

"No," Moss says. "I'd go *anywhere* but here."

My head bobs along with Moss's. "Is that why you run so much?"

"My ticket out of here is a college scholarship. My mom sure as hell can't afford to pay."

All of the words coming out of Moss's mouth—I want to catch them and save them in my pocket. "Color told me about the Blockbuster."

"I knew my mom would do it eventually, but Color's more of a dreamer than I am." Moss dips his chin in the water. "Which means life disappoints her more often."

I understand that, but right now, swimming in a cool river with a boy who tempted me to leave my fears behind me, life is kind of amazing.

"What does your intuition say about how deep it is here?" I ask.

Moss is contemplative before he says, "It's telling me twelve feet."

"We should put your intuition to the test." When he returns the smile plastered on my face, I hear the crank of the roller coaster inching up a really big hill. I feel it in my belly. Like sunlight just wrapped around my insides and gave them a really big, almost suffocating hug.

"We should," he says.

We disappear below the water. Deeper and deeper, I pull myself, looking for the bottom.

Complex Math Problem: If the world is round, is the bottom really the bottom, or are we really just searching for someone else's sky?

Moss and I surface at the same time, gasping for air, my lungs tight. "It's . . ." Moss gasps. "Deeper . . ." Gasp. "Than . . . I thought." Gasp.

It's then that I realize that Moss is right in front of me. Like *right* in front of me. His nose inches from mine. His lips, which he licks droplets of water from, are just as close. His legs swim in between my legs, his arms tangle in the waves my arms make. And in just a second, he'll realize how close we are and back away.

One, one thousand.

Two, one thousand.

Three, one thousand.

Moss hasn't backed away from me.

His hand comes out of the water and touches my bottom lip. "You're turning blue, Esther."

That's funny. Because I thought I was just turning *on*. Back on after months of being off. Moss's leg comes in between mine, and lifts me up by my seat to keep me above the water. I didn't realize I was sinking. I thought I was floating just then. I think the rose quartz Dharma gave Moss is working.

"This was a good idea," I say.

"I'm full of them," he says.

And, by God, I believe him.

25

I think my fish might be depressed. I'm not sure how much longer I can keep her in the fishbowl. I ask the guy at the pet store, and he says, "Is it swimming around?"

"Yes."

"Blowing bubbles?"

"Yes."

"Then it's fine. You'll know when it's depressed."

"How?" I ask.

"It'll float."

I'm not sure why I ask this guy anything. He keeps canaries in a cage. Everyone knows why the caged bird sings. It wants to get the hell out of there.

I tell him he should let the birds go, but he disagrees. "As long as they're in the cage, I keep them alive. I keep them safe." He points out the window. "Out there . . . Who knows what would happen?"

I leave then, because this guy is the worst kind of liar. Plus, we're taking Beth to Heaven for the first time tonight, to celebrate Christmas, even though the actual holiday isn't for a few more days. Color's mom promised she wouldn't sell the place until after the New Year.

It didn't take long for me to figure out what presents I was going to get everyone, and I want this night to be special. Last year, my pregnancy forced everyone home and into hiding for the entire holiday season. Mom didn't even want to go to the supermarket, so we ordered pizza on Christmas Day, and Tom made me hide upstairs when it was delivered. God forbid Domino's figured out I was pregnant.

I put on the dress Mom bought me a few months ago. It's supposed to fit me by now, even though it's a summer dress. We are, after all, in the midst of a heat wave.

I can practically hear the zipper whining, barely holding itself together. It's tired of being pulled so damn tight. But it's closed and should do the job for tonight.

Before leaving my room, I come eye to eye with my fish. I can tell she wants out of her bowl. She's getting bigger. Soon enough, she'll outgrow me, and I'll be forced to let her go, though I hope I have the strength to set her free before then.

Mom makes some casserole thing for dinner, with "hidden vegetables" that aren't so hidden, and Tom and I pretend not to taste them. The table has transformed from a cornucopia of Thanksgiving gourds to candles that smell like pine trees, cranberries, and mistletoe. It will stay decorated like this until the New Year. We're pretending we live in a place where it might snow on Christmas. Mom has the twenty-four-hour Christmas radio station playing all day every day. Presently, we're listening to the Mannheim Steamroller version of "Deck the Halls." I want to steamroll myself.

Hannah isn't subject to this holiday charade tonight. She's at church. She was picked by Ms. Sylvia for an elite group of singers that will start preparing for Easter's big Passion play. Beth said they've never done that in the past, but luckily, she and I weren't asked to be in this group.

Mom makes comments about how good the dress looks on me, how my figure is coming back, how it took her forever to lose the baby weight, but when you're young it's so much easier. I want to gag on the hidden vegetables.

Instead I blurt out, "The perks of being a teen mom!"

Tom drops his fork and splatters hidden vegetables all over his tie. "Darn it all to heck." He really wants to say something else, and we all know it. He wipes the food from his tie, takes it off, and hands it to Mom, who's waiting with club soda to get any stains out.

"Sorry," Mom says.

The doorbell saves me from apologizing, which I don't want to do anyway.

"Who's that?" Tom asks.

"Beth."

Mom chokes and squeaks and spills club soda. "Beth?"

What I want to say is, *Yes, Mom, I'm saving you from lying. From this moment forward, there will be one less lie in the universe . . . even if Beth is really here to take me to Heaven so I can be with friends you don't want to recognize.*

I let Beth in the door and introduce her to Tom. The whole time she does the cross-grab thing she always does. Tom totally notices and looks at Beth approvingly. If he only knew he was meeting a lesbian who drove me to Albuquerque to see a psychic.

With Tom satisfied and his tie saved from stains, Beth and I leave. Mom stops me before I get out the front door.

"That dress really does look great on you. I'm proud of you, Esther."

"Are you proud of me because I don't look like I had a baby anymore, and now everyone can stop worrying people will find out? Or are you proud of me because I've made friends who care about me?"

Mom smiles. "Be home by ten."

She trades one lie for another.

∞

Heaven is a Christmas extravaganza. Twinkling lights dangle across the ceiling, and there's even a Christmas tree with a train. It looks old-fashioned and homey and perfect. For a second, I almost think I smell snow.

139

"This place is amazing," Beth says, looking around. She lights up in Heaven, too.

Color has the same radio station playing that was on at my house, but because it's coming through an old radio, it crackles with static, and Color has to keep adjusting the antenna. The songs sound better, more authentic, in Heaven.

Jesús is wearing a hat with mistletoe dangling from it. When he comes up to me, the mistletoe hangs over my head, and he says, "It's tradition."

I wrap my arms around his neck and kiss him on the lips. When I pull back, I notice he has bags under his eyes.

"Are you OK?" I touch them.

"Just a little tired from work." He walks over to Moss. "Fungus?"

Moss actually laughs as he gives Jesús a kiss on the cheek.

"What about me?" Beth asks. Jesús doesn't leave her out. She gives him the longest kiss of all of us, and when she pulls back, she says, "Sorry. It's been a while."

And Jesús says, "Excuse me while I sit down and wait for my third arm to go away."

Heaven smells like cinnamon and candy canes and love. I inhale and feel myself filling up, all bubbly.

With my gifts set under the tree, Moss squats down next to me.

"You know, you didn't have to get gifts."

"Is this when you say, 'you're gift enough for us, Esther'?" I laugh. Moss doesn't.

"Something like that." He winks, and I'm left to swim in his words. Except this time there's no water to cool me down. I heat up all the way to the tips of my earlobes.

I show Beth the wall of lost things in the porn section, and she's as entranced with it as I was. It's not every day you see walls come alive with complete chaos. Beth takes her necklace off and tacks it to the wall.

"Really?" I say, concerned. "She's lost?"

"Brittany hasn't emailed me in months. It's not looking good." Beth shrugs. "It's OK. She lives in Oregon. Long distance never works."

"Well, she's in good company now." I touch the cross on the wall.

Color pops a bottle of champagne, and we pass it around. It goes straight to my head. I think I'm living in bubbles tonight. Everything is just so light. Even the heavy air feels weightless.

When it's time to open presents, we all sit around the Christmas tree, illuminated by twinkle lights. I don't know if I've ever been this happy. I don't know if I've ever been this complete. And the strangest thing happens in the middle of my happiness—I worry it will all go away.

I look at the tree and wonder if happiness really is infinite. What if all this disappears?

I was happy before, in Ohio, and it left like snow in the spring. Is happiness like water—sometimes a solid, sometimes a liquid, and sometimes a vapor?

I was in love with Amit, and now I can't stop thinking about Moss. It used to be Amit's hands I wanted to feel, Amit's mouth I wanted to taste. Now my eyes keep wandering to Moss's fingers, Moss's lips. It's all changed so rapidly, and yet a few months ago, I thought my life might never change.

I force myself not to think about that because it's ruining the moment.

Jesús gives me my very own coffee mug that says: YOU + ME = <3. "Get it?" he says. "Since you love math?" I almost cry. Jesús says he'll keep it at HuggaMug for me. He says we'll call it "The Cup of Life," since coffee brought me back to life.

"No, you did," I say to him, and he blushes.

Beth gives me a pitch pipe. "It's a joke. Because you're always off-key when you sing." It's so Beth that I can't help but launch myself on her for a hug.

Moss hands me a box. I wasn't expecting anything from him, and he must be able to read my face, because he says, "Go on. Open it."

I do and gasp, looking at him. He offers a devilish wink in return.

"What is it?" Jesús asks.

"Yeah, Esther. What is it?" Moss taunts.

It's a bathing suit, a freaking two-piece bathing suit that I will never wear, but I will keep for the rest of my life, because *wow*. If Moss still wants me to hate him, he's doing a really bad job of it.

"Nothing," I say, closing the box at once.

I try to distract them by handing out my gifts.

Jesús shakes his present and tears into the wrapping. "Mon chéri!" he says when he sees what's inside. He puts on the black beret and scarf, dramatically tossing the scarf over his shoulder. It looks perfect on him. Very French. "Now that I have a new hat, you need this." Jesús puts the mistletoe hat on my head and kisses me.

Beth opens her gift next. It's a T-shirt that says: LET US PAUSE NOW FOR A MOMENT OF SCIENCE. She puts it on over the shirt she's wearing, which says: GO JESUS, IT'S YOUR BIRTHDAY. With a hug, she says, "Hashtag. I love it."

I give Moss his gift next. It rattles when he shakes it. Moss cocks his head at me.

"Open it," I say.

He pulls back the wrapping paper to expose a box of blue tacks.

"Blue?" he says.

"Red for the places you need to go. Blue for the places you've been."

Moss's gray eyes get all intense, and I remember swimming together in the Rio Grande. How his legs tangled with mine. How water seemed to dangle on his lips like it knew how wonderful it is to linger there. How we were swimming in the truth at that very moment. My body covers in tingles when Moss says, "Thank you, Esther."

"You're welcome, Moss." But really I should be thanking him, because I am on fire. All over. And what I really mean is—you are welcome, Moss. To me.

I give Color her gift. She turns the box around in her hands and then presses it to her forehead, right on her third eye. "I already know I'm going to love it." When she opens it and finds a Magic 8 Ball, she squeals, "I was right! I do love it!"

"In case your intuition ever breaks down," I say.

"We need to put it to the test." Color gestures for us all to huddle in close. "Everyone think of a question."

She passes the Magic 8 Ball to Jesús.

"Will Brett ever realize he's gay and in love with me?" he says and shakes it. The answer pops up, and Jesús groans. "Not likely."

He tosses the Magic 8 Ball to Moss, who asks, "Will Jesús and Color ever realize that moss is not a fungus, it's a plant?" He shakes the ball, and we wait for the answer. Moss exhales. "My sources say no."

"The Magic 8 Ball never lies, Fungus," Jesús says.

Defeated, Moss gives it to Beth. She asks, "Will I ever walk on the moon?" She waits for the answer patiently. "It is certain!" she exclaims.

She passes the Magic 8 Ball to Color, who spins it around in her hands, feeling it from every side. "Will we ever meet our dad?" She looks at Moss as she waits for the answer. "Cannot predict right now." With a shrug, she says, "It was worth a shot." Then she hands the Magic 8 Ball to me.

All the answers swim around inside as I roll it.

Would Amit be mad if I moved on?

Has *he* moved on?

Should I kiss Moss?

What is Hannah lying about?

Where is my dad?

Does he think about me?

And what about California? Why can't I stop thinking about it? Why did I have to see that psychic in the first place? Does getting one answer just mean you get more questions? Why is nothing concrete?

Are the answers really right here in my hand?

I shake the Magic 8 Ball and ask, "Will Tom ever fill our empty pool?" An answer swims to the surface. "Ask again later."

∞

Color doesn't give me a gift. I try not to act disappointed when everyone else gets one. I take an extra swig of champagne to wash down the icky feeling.

But if I'm being honest, I'm disappointed.

At the end of the night, Moss stands in the porn section, staring at the map of India on the wall. He's got the box of blue tacks in his hand. By the look on his face, he's desperate to use one—to go somewhere and document it with a tack.

I stand next to him as he stares at the map. We don't say anything for a bit, and then I take a blue tack out of his box, and Moss says, "I thought they were all mine."

I cup it in my hand, a surreptitious grin forming, and shrug. It's my turn to be the silent one again.

"You're still wearing the mistletoe hat," Moss says.

I glance up and catch sight of the green leaves dangling from my head. My stomach plummets to my toes. I forgot. Moss is now hovering over me, just like the mistletoe.

"Does that mean I have to kiss you, Esther?"

It takes a moment for words to come, but slowly I manage to whisper, "I'd prefer you kiss me when you *want* to."

Color finds us in the porn section standing still, covered in innuendo. She coughs, a knowing grin pulling at her cheeks. Moss and I step back, the mistletoe no longer lingering between us.

"Don't worry," Color says. "I didn't forget about you, Esther. I have a Christmas gift, but it won't be here until after the New Year."

"OK." I tear my eyes off Moss, knowing that pieces of me will continue to be acutely aware of his presence, even when I'm not looking at him.

"You just have to promise me that you'll use it," Color says.

"Well, what is it?"

Color shakes her head, her smile unmoved. "Just trust me. Do you promise?"

And because I don't think I trust anyone more than Color, I say, "I promise."

26

Aunt Emily comes for Christmas bearing homemade gifts and memories from Ohio. It sets Tom on edge because Aunt Emily likes wine, and wine makes Mom remember who she used to be. I've seen it. After a few drinks, Mom will be cursing like a sailor and talking about getting drunk in high school.

Aunt Emily gives Hannah and me matching shirts that Mom says we *must* wear to the Christmas Eve service at church, where the youth choir is performing "modern Christmas classics" like Coldplay's "Christmas Lights" and the Killers' "Boots." *Classics.*

After the service is over, Beth, who's wearing the T-shirt I gave her, asks Mom and Tom if I can sleep over at her house for New Year's Eve.

Mom says, "Well . . . I don't . . ."

But Tom says, "I think that's a great idea."

And when Beth walks away, Tom says, "That Beth looks like a good Christian girl."

Aunt Emily says, "I thought good Christians didn't judge people on their looks," and Mom tells Aunt Emily to curb her attitude.

Tom sends me to look for Hannah, who hasn't appeared since the end of the service. I check in the choir room, the sanctuary, the bathroom. I go back down the Sunday school hallway that's manic with parents picking up kids. It is definitely a wrong turn. I have to get out of there now because the sound of crying babies makes my heart ache and my belly tight. And all I think is, *California, California, California. It ends at the ocean.*

But what does? I don't know. There are too many questions and not enough Magic 8 Balls.

I run down the hallway like a lunatic, feeling the past chasing me. I can't afford to drown in memories here, among the Christians. It's safer drowning in an empty pool. I'm ruined for babysitting for the rest of my youth.

I swing around the corner at full speed, my arms flapping at my side. I'm a nonrunner who's running, all awkward, bouncing body parts. How does Moss do this with his third arm?

I stop to heave and maybe die on the floor, when Hannah rounds the corner with a giddy expression on her face. When she sees me, the giddiness dries up.

"What are you doing?"

"Dying," I say between pinched breaths. "Just . . . dying . . . I'll . . . be . . . fine."

"Put your arms over your head."

I do that, and it's oddly helpful.

"Were you . . ." I heave. "With Peter?"

But Hannah doesn't answer because all of her attention goes to Pastor Rick, who's just come down the hallway.

"Twins!" he yells when he sees us. I'd forgotten that Hannah and I are wearing matching homemade shirts.

"We are *so* not twins," Hannah says, and all the help she just offered is washed away. She sounds disgusted at the possibility that we could remotely look alike.

"He's talking about our shirts." *Asshole.* I want to put that at the end of the sentence. *Asshole.*

I walk away from Hannah and Pastor Rick. I don't care where Hannah goes or if she is ever found. She's on her own from this point forward.

∞

I overhear Mom and Aunt Emily talking in the kitchen that night. It's Christmas Eve and I'm supposed to be sleeping because "Santa comes tomorrow." Mom still says things like that. I mean, I had a freaking baby, and she still says "baby" things to me. It feels odd.

But then again, I keep thinking about the houses hosting Christmas parties with eggnog and oysters Rockefeller, where people stand around a piano and sing Christmas carols. And snow. Lots of snow. Snow that comes from clouds and covers lawns in a white blanket where you can make a million snow angels.

Houses like the one we had in Ohio. Houses filled with love, even if it's just fake love for one night. Christmas Eve is the one day when everyone wants to be Christian because it feels good. Even me. Because a baby was born this night in Bethlehem. And people love babies, especially baby Jesus.

But here's the thing—Mary got pregnant out of wedlock. She and Joseph had to do a rush job on their wedding so Mary didn't look like a whore, because even back then a woman was either a whore or a virgin. The rules still applied to Mary, even though she was carrying the Son of God. That's the plight of women—no matter how miraculous we are, we still have to live in a world governed by men's standards.

I stare at my female fish and wonder why God picked a woman out of wedlock. Why put her through that? Where's the grace in that? Why must it always be women who carry the burden? If we're that much better than men, why didn't Mary have a girl? Why wasn't it the Daughter of God?

My fish seems to say, *Look it up in the Bible if you're that interested.*

But I'm not that interested. Men wrote the Bible anyway. No wonder Jesus was a boy.

Even knowing that, Christmas Eve is still getting to me right now. It's a holiday about a baby, and so I can't stop thinking about my baby. The need to cry at any second will go away in a few days, just like everyone pretending to be Christian tonight will forget to go to church next Sunday.

Tiptoeing toward the kitchen for a snack, I stop when I hear Mom and Aunt Emily, who's working on her current knitting project. She brings it everywhere. I think Aunt Emily has busy hands, and if she's not doing something, she gets caught up in stuff she shouldn't.

Aunt Emily puts the knitting down.

"This doesn't seem right, Julie," she says. "It's so flipping dry here. Move back to Ohio."

"We can't." Mom fills a glass of water. "Drink this. It will help."

"Water isn't the solution." But Aunt Emily chugs the whole glass anyway. "We have plenty of water in Ohio. We have a damn lake full of it."

"Just drop it, Em. It's not happening."

"It's because of Tom." Aunt Emily picks up her knitting again and starts in on the sock she's making. She doesn't look at Mom when she says, "I warned you about him."

"He's a good man." Mom rubs her temples. "Better than most, actually."

"I know you got a raw deal with Rob. I could kill that bastard for leaving you alone with two kids."

"Tom would never leave." Mom must be desperate because she opens a bottle of wine and pours two glasses.

"I know," Aunt Emily says. "But that doesn't mean you should stay."

Mom takes a large gulp. "I'm staying, God damn it. Good enough is good enough."

Aunt Emily downs half her glass of wine and then motions for Mom to refill. "I just don't think you need to run from the past anymore. It's done."

"You know as well as I do—the past is never done." Mom tops off her glass and drinks some, then fills it again. "It will never go away, Em. For the rest of her life. It will never go away."

It's then that I realize Mom isn't thinking about herself. She's thinking about me.

27

Jesús is sleeping in the laundromat. While riding my bike past it, I notice his red, run-down ten-speed parked out front and see him through the windows. He's spread out on the chairs, his head cradled in his arms. He's the only person here. When I walk inside and the door dings, he doesn't even stir.

He's wearing the same thing he wore to our Christmas celebration in Heaven, complete with the scarf and beret. The December heat wave finally left, and the weather is acting appropriately again. The nights are chilly. If I lie outside in the pool and close my eyes, I can almost smell snow. Almost. But the days heat up again, and the desert acts like the desert, and my cactus thrives.

I sit down next to Jesús and watch him sleep as laundry tumbles in the washers and dryers.

> Complex Math Problem: If one sock is left behind at the laundromat, does it become single, or is it forever looking for its original mate? Or does it find another mate that may not match perfectly, because good enough is good enough?

Is good enough really good enough?

When I look at Jesús, I know I want better than good for him. I want great. I want amazingness. I want him to be so loved he can barely stand it.

Why is it so easy to want love for other people but not to accept it for ourselves?

Last year at school, a guidance counselor came to speak to all the freshman classes about hormones and sex and love and respect. She said, "Imagine you have a best friend who talks to you the way you talk to yourself. Raise your hand if you would be friends with that person?" No one raised a hand. Not even the popular people who seemed like they had it all together. No one.

Jesús wakes up, completely surprised to see me sitting at his feet. He sits up swiftly, yawning and adjusting the beret.

"Mon chéri, what are you doing here?"

"I saw you through the window."

He looks tired. Maybe one step beyond tired. Exhausted. He says, "The washer at my house is broken."

"Oh."

"That's why I'm here."

"OK."

"Because it's broken."

"I hate when things break," I say.

"Me, too."

The clothes tumble in the washing machines, tossed this way and that, as Jesús and I watch. Five minutes remain until they're done.

"You know what I've always wanted to do?" I say.

"What?"

I push the laundry cart back and forth on its wheels. "Ride in one of these things."

We smile simultaneously, and then, because we're alone in a laundromat and no one is looking, I climb into the basket. Jesús pushes me around the whole place, the warm, fabric-softener-infused wind blowing back my hair. He spins me in circles as I hold on tightly, screaming, "I'm so dizzy! This is awesome!"

I make Jesús take a ride and spin him around until he says, "I'm going to vomit *Exorcist*-style all over the place!"

When he's done spinning, Jesús doesn't look as exhausted anymore. He switches his clothes from the washer to the dryer, and we sit down and watch them tumble in a circle.

"The humming of the machines always makes me tired." Jesús rubs his eyes. "I can't help but fall asleep."

I slouch back in the seat. The laundry swirls and swirls. Jesús leans into me and yawns.

"I'm just so tired," he says, and I can tell by his tone that he means tired with life. Because things break too often, and you find yourself at the laundromat with so many abandoned socks it's overwhelming.

"Here." I make him rest his head on my shoulder. "You can sleep on me."

"Thanks, mon chéri. You make a good place to rest." Jesús falls back asleep soon after. I watch his laundry dry and hope all of his socks match, and that the washer at his house gets fixed soon. I never have to worry about my laundry. Mom does it. She carries the burden of lost socks all on her own.

I shouldn't be so hard on her. It's no wonder she thinks good enough is good enough.

28

New Year's Eve in Heaven is depressing. Color's mom says she can't delay any longer. She needs to sell the Blockbuster now, so the garage sale is tomorrow. Color and Moss spent the whole afternoon putting price tags on everything.

"But how can I really put a price on this stuff?" Color asks me. "It means more than money to me."

"Just remember, it's a rebirth. This isn't over," I say, half to her and half to myself.

I take one final perusal of everything.

Pogo stick $10

Tricycle $15

Oversized chair with stains $20

VCR with tapes included $20

"What about the family pictures?" I ask.

Color shows me a bin of empty frames. Each one is priced at a dollar. "I kept all the pictures. I just can't sell them. They're like . . ."

"Family?" I ask.

Color snaps her fingers. "Yes. Family."

She has all of my old stuff priced out, too. My old hat and matching gloves are five dollars. The winter coat I wore in eighth grade is seven dollars.

"I don't know if I can stay here all night. It's like sleeping in a graveyard," Moss says.

The plan was to spend the last seconds of the year in Heaven. Mom and Tom think I'm sleeping over at Beth's. Beth's parents know we're sleeping in Heaven, because Beth is the only person I know who doesn't lie. She told them the truth, and they think it's kind of cool.

But right now, it doesn't feel cool. Moss is right. It feels like a graveyard. And Color just seems so depressed.

"Let's go somewhere," I say.

"Yes!" Color perks up. "Where?"

"I have my parents' car, so I can drive," Beth offers.

Where should a group of teenagers go in Truth or Consequences on New Year's Eve? The blue tack I took from Moss is in my pocket. I brought it just in case . . .

"I know," I say. At that, everyone's face lights up, waiting for the answer. Their light makes me so bright, I might break into little stars. "Let's go to Mexico."

∞

The night is dark and chilly. After more than two hours of driving, we arrive at our destination. We stand at the border of New Mexico and Mexico. I wrap my arms around my waist, staring at the land in front of me.

"What exactly are we doing here?" Jesús asks.

"Looking," Color says.

"Why?" Jesús asks.

"Because we can," she says.

And Beth says, "I can't believe I haven't done this before."

"It's right there?" Moss asks, looking at me, his eyes so bright with excitement it hurts, but in the best way.

"Right there," I say. "A whole other country."

"I knew Mexico was close, but I didn't know it was this close," Color says.

"New Mexico." Jesús points at the ground and then gestures off in the distance. "Old Mexico."

"Real Mexico," Moss says in awe.

The road we drove down is dusty and not paved. We're still in the desert. Dried, leafless bushes and cacti are the only plant life that live here, and even then, I'm not sure it's living. It's a playground for snakes and scorpions. Everything has to fight so hard to stay alive when there's so little actually living. But right now—I feel vibrant. I feel like I'm living for everything around me, so the plants and animals can survive. I'm happy to live and breathe for them because life is so good.

"What should we do?" Beth asks.

"I don't know," Jesús says.

"Look at it and ponder the numinous," Color says. She wraps her arm around Beth. "Isn't it crazy that another country is so close, and yet we can never go there because we're not allowed? But it's all land. I mean, men created the border, not nature. Nature doesn't discriminate. Men do. It's like we're boxed in, but we do it to ourselves. We imprison each other with lines and boundaries instead of just letting people be free."

"You've gone down the rabbit hole again, my friend," Jesús says.

"Can I touch it?" Beth walks up to the run-down barbed-wire fence that lines the border.

"Just be careful," Jesús says. "Once you touch it, you might want to go to the other side, and then what if we can't get you back? You'll be lost forever."

"That's just what society wants you to think." Color shakes her head. "It's just a line. You won't be lost. We can still see you. Touching it might just set you free."

"God, I love all this talk of touching," Jesús says. "Say 'touch' again."

"Touch." Color smiles. Jesús bites on his fist.

Silently, Moss stands next to me, as usual, but also *not* so usual because his silence in the past has been coated in something darker. But not right now. Right now—he feels light. He feels like he's really living, too.

"I can't believe you did this," he says.

I shrug. "I didn't do anything."

Moss steps closer to me, our pinkies touching, warm skin to warm skin, and whispers, "Don't lie, Esther."

"Don't lie, Esther." Amit said that once. He was wearing navy-blue shorts and a yellow T-shirt—our gym uniform—but neither of us was very good at gym.

"It's for the best. This has to end." I went over exactly what I was going to say at the breakfast table that morning. I even practiced in the mirror.

"For the best?" Amit said.

"It's the only solution," I rephrased. Tom said that at one point.

"Some problems have multiple solutions, Esther."

"I know that." That wasn't part of the script I rehearsed. I also knew that Tom was solving the problem for himself. I pressed on, though. "But not this time."

"But what about . . . us? I'm the variable. I need my coefficient."

"We were wrong," I said. Mom's and Tom's words. Not mine. But I borrowed them for the moment.

"Love isn't wrong," Amit said.

I knew there was no going back. That's not how time works. It moves forward, like everything else.

"It's over," I said, and with that one sentence, it was.

But I never thought I'd move on. Just because something is over doesn't mean a person lets go. But when I look down at the hand closest to mine, it's not Amit's I'm imagining anymore. My memories of him are finding their way back to where they belong . . . in the past.

I never thought I'd be ready, until this moment, right now, when I find myself standing on the border next to a boy, ready to take a leap.

I'm breathless when I say to Moss, "OK. I won't lie. I did this for you."

Beth inspects the barbed-wire fence. "I wonder if it's electrified." She picks up a rock and throws it at the wire. Nothing happens, so she tries again. Still nothing. "I think it's just a run-down fence."

"Well, should we?" I ask the group, but really I'm asking Moss. Should we? Can we? Is this real?

"It's definitely illegal," Beth says.

"And probably not the best idea," Jesús says.

"But it's just so close," Color offers.

And Moss says, "Do you have that blue tack, Esther?"

I take it out of my pocket and show it to him. "Let's go to Mexico," I say.

We cross the border, climbing over the fence together. Within moments, we're standing in another country, looking back at New Mexico, our footprints on the other side.

"What do we do now?" Jesús asks.

"Ponder the numinous," Color says.

"The numinous seems to be everywhere," Jesús says. We all stand in the quiet of Mexico for a while. The stars are the same. They shine on us as we stare at where we were just moments earlier, just across the border.

"Do you ever wonder why you were born right here, right now?" Beth asks.

"I wonder all the time why I was born gay." Jesús picks up a rock and tosses it back into the United States. "One small move . . . and that rock is now an American rock."

"Or is it just pretending?" Beth offers. "It will always be Mexican, no matter where it lives. You can't make a Mexican rock change just by moving it."

"Now that's the numinous," Jesús says.

The five of us stand still, looking at the United States just feet away, like we're waiting for something to happen. The wind doesn't even make a sound.

"I don't feel any different in Mexico," Color says.

"Me neither," Beth says.

Jesús says, "Let's go home. Mexico is boring." He carefully climbs over the fence, but Moss and I stay.

"Esther," he whispers.

"Yeah, Moss."

His fingers interlace with mine, the feeling startling me, but only for a moment. Then my palm settles into Moss's palm like I fit there perfectly. Like this is where I belong. I never thought I'd feel this again.

"Come on, you lovebirds!" Jesús hollers over his shoulder from America. But Moss and I are in Mexico right now, and I'm not ready to leave. Mexico is amazing. Just give us one more second that goes on for infinity.

Moss looks down at his hand interlaced with mine that, in the darkness, look like one unit—pressed together. He says, "I guess I like surprises after all."

And I say, "Thank God."

∞

We drive back to Truth or Consequences. It's almost midnight. A new year in New Mexico. Touchdown Jesus is one of the only lit-up things in town.

"I've always wanted to try to climb up Scary Jesus and make friends with him," Color says. "Then maybe he won't be scary anymore."

"Why don't we?" Beth says.

"Seriously?" Color sits up excited in the car. "I love you, Beth."

Beth blushes as she pulls into the parking lot of the church, and we all get out of the car.

Jesús walks right up to the gigantic Touchdown Jesus and pats it. "Jesus, it's nice to meet you. I'm Jesus but with flair."

Color inspects the statue, pushing on it and patting it to make sure it's safe to climb, but it's a gigantic Jesus statue—nothing feels safe about this.

"Someone give me a lift." Color holds her foot out, and Beth gives her a boost. The night air is chilly, making me shiver, and the next thing I know, Moss is running his hands up and down my arms to keep me warm, his chest so close to my back that the heat radiating off him hums straight into my heart.

"OK?" he asks.

I offer Moss a grin that whispers yes as Color makes it to the top of the Touchdown Jesus. Yeah, this is OK. This is better than OK. Even with gigantic Jesus watching.

"It's so beautiful up here!" she hollers down at us.

Beth climbs up next, and then Jesús. Then Moss makes a cup with his hand and gives me a boost. He climbs up last, and then we're all standing in the palm of Touchdown Jesus, looking out at Truth or Consequences.

"It *is* beautiful," Beth says.

"All it took was climbing into the palm of Jesus for me to no longer be afraid of him," Color says. "That's poetic."

"I guess things aren't so scary when you really look at it," I say.

Jesús reaches his arms out. "It's almost like I'm flying."

I stretch out my arms, just like Jesús, like a bird, and let the wind rush through my fingers. "From up here, it almost seems possible," I say.

"What does?" Moss asks.

"Everything." I smile at him, and he offers the same expression back to me.

"It's even better when you close your eyes," Jesús says, flapping his arms.

Color does the same, pumping her arms. "Happy New Year, Truth or Consequences!" she yells at the top of her lungs.

We all holler back. "Happy New Year!" Our voices echo in the vacant desert.

When we're done flying, we all lie down in the palm of Jesus, our heads next to each other, looking up at the stars. And right now, somehow, time and borders don't seem to exist. It isn't a new year or a new day or a new minute. It just is. We just are.

With all of us together, infinity forms out of nothing.

∞

Moss looks at me intently. Jesús is asleep on the other side of me. Somehow on the last night of Heaven, we've found our way into the palm of Touchdown Jesus instead.

"Happy New Year, Esther," he whispers, brushing my hair from my forehead with cool fingertips.

"Happy New Year, Moss."

"Thank you for taking me to Mexico."

"You're welcome."

And he says, "Am I? Welcome?"

I lean in and kiss him. Our cold lips touch and melt together. And in this moment, I feel the past evaporate, even if only for just a moment.

Love *is* like water. Sometimes it's as solid as a kiss. Sometimes it's as changing as the Rio Grande. And sometimes it's as invisible as the steam that disappears from a cup of coffee.

When I pull back from Moss's lips, heat still connecting the air between us, he says, "I guess I got my answer."

29

It's January. School has started again, and I'm jealous that Color, Moss, Jesús, and Beth get to see each other every day, while I still lie in my empty pool when they're not around.

Color made over three thousand dollars at the garage sale, and the very next day, her mom put up the FOR SALE sign. Now Color sets brushes, rollers, and two containers of paint on the ground outside of Blockbuster.

"This place needs to sell." Color holds up a paintbrush. "It's time to cover up Heaven."

"How can you be so calm about this?" I ask.

Jesús pats me gently on the shoulder. "In the end, it's just walls, mon chéri."

"And you know how I feel about walls," Color says. "They crumble anyway." That's why she has glow-in-the-dark stars on her ceiling. But I can tell by how she says it that Color's as sad as I am. Some walls can hold you together when no one else does.

Inside, everything is gone. The room looks so big and empty now. The concrete makes the air cold, and I shiver. Moss comes to stand close behind, offering his heat where mine has gone.

Maybe it's not as cold as it was a second ago.

Only one thing remains. Color pulls back the curtain to the porn section. The wall of lost items is still here, so many words coloring the space. My throat starts to tighten at the thought of painting over all of this beauty. Where will it go?

Color pops the lid on the paint can before anyone can say anything else. "My mom said I should use white paint, but I just couldn't. As a society, we can't be afraid of some color." She has picked out a sky blue to paint over the walls.

"Yes, but it's easier when things are black-and-white," Jesús says as he spreads sheets over the ground.

"Who said life should be easy?" Color asks. "Where's the fun in that?"

I stand in front of my word. The nurse's voice echoes in my head.

Beth stands next to me. "How do you know she went to a family in California?"

"My mom told me."

"Did she tell you anything else? Like what adoption agency she used?"

"She said Tom made sure the baby was going to a good Christian family." I turn to face Beth. "I hope she ended up with parents like yours, not mine."

But Beth seems to be thinking so hard that my compliment doesn't even register. "And did you sign the birth certificate?"

"No way," I say. "My mom had power of attorney. She signed."

"What's your mom's first name again?"

"Julie."

"Julie," Beth repeats.

"Yeah," I say.

"Julie signed the birth certificate."

"Yes," I say, noticing Beth's thinking face. "Why?"

Beth snaps out of it. "I'm just wondering."

Color wraps an arm around my shoulder then, and says, "Will you do the honors, Esther?" A paintbrush drips sky-blue paint onto the sheets. "I don't think I can do it."

Every person in the room has helped me, so I take the paintbrush from Color, walk up to the wall, and say, "It's not really going away. We're just covering it up. It will always be here. For infinity."

"I love infinity," Color says.

And Jesús says, "Amen."

And Moss says, "Just do it, Esther."

Beth is concentrating on something in her head. She barely notices what's going on.

I know this moment isn't a complex problem that needs to be solved. It just is. Sometimes you have to paint the walls and start over. Heaven isn't what's held on the walls anyway. It's inside the person who holds the paintbrush.

∞

Beth tells me she doesn't want her necklace back, to just paint it to the wall. When all is said and done, the only thing left in Heaven is Beth's cross, permanently stuck to the wall painted the color of the sky.

30

Moss is supposed to be at HuggaMug, but Jesús said he would cover the shift by himself. Color is cleaning someone's house. Beth is who knows where, and I'm supposed to be at the pet store. Instead, Moss's feet are tangled with mine. His room is clean, like it always is, but his bed is messy, because we've been rolling around on it for the past hour, kissing.

"Let's go to Africa," Moss says.

"OK."

"Or Alaska. I want to go to Alaska."

"OK." My head swims. I can't see straight.

"Anywhere with water. Have you ever noticed how moss doesn't grow in the desert? For once in my life, I want to know what it feels like to be surrounded by water."

"OK," I say dreamily. This is the most he's ever talked.

"Tell me another math joke."

"Why didn't the quarter roll down the hill with the nickel?"

"Why?"

"Because it had more cents."

He laughs into my neck, and I melt into the bed in a pile of happiness.

"Tell me another one."

"What do you call friends who love math?" I ask, my voice quivering from his whisper on my neck.

"What?" Moss murmurs again. His breath is so warm, I think my skin might be on fire. Bliss surrounds me, covering me, waving over my head to my feet. I want him to kiss me again, to lay his body on top of mine and cover me, just like happiness is right now.

"Algebros."

"Are we algebros?" he asks.

"Nooooooooo."

"No?" He pulls back and looks at me.

"I think we're beyond algebros. You gave me a bathing suit for Christmas."

"You gave me Mexico," he whispers. I glance at the map on his wall with all the red tacks. The single blue one stands out. I kiss Moss fiercely then. I've restrained myself up until this point, but my strength is waning.

"OK," he says, breathless. Moss licks his lips like he wants to taste what's left of me there. "If we aren't algebros—are we talking calculus? Trig?"

"Shut up." I pull him down on top of me.

Moss's fingers press into the vertebrae of my lower spine, like he's playing keys on a piano, softly, investigating my body. His fingers climb higher up my back, and shivers cascade down my body. Holy lightheadedness.

I kiss him more and pull him closer, my legs holding him to me. Moss's fingers grace my hair.

His lips feel good. Better than good. Amazing. Foreign. New. I never thought I'd like new, but new is good. New Mexico is good. I'm along for this ride wherever it goes. Somehow, I didn't wilt and die in the desert, like I thought I would. I've figured out how to live.

I pull Moss closer to me, my hands finding their way under his shirt. I don't want to let go.

"Esther?"

And for the first time in my life, I say, "No questions."

There's just so much more to explore. And if Moss can't go to Alaska right now, maybe we can discover other things right here, right now, that are just as good, an adventure of body and being. Places you can only find when you stop and explore what's right in front of you.

I hold Moss to me and kiss him. Our chests press to each other, as if we're folding together. My tongue explores every inch of his mouth. I need to taste what's inside—all the words and thoughts he never says. They're there, waiting for me. I just need to find my way through his maze.

"Esther," Moss says in my ear. "We can slow down."

But I kiss him again, because less talking, more making out. All I know right now is that this feels good.

"Esther," Moss says. "We need to stop."

"Why?" I say, breathless.

Moss pulls away hastily. "Because I hear someone coming."

I scramble back from him, but there's nowhere for me to hide. Moss's bedroom door opens, and we face his mom, who's holding a basket full of laundry.

"Oh no." She drops the basket and covers her eyes. Clothes fall all over the clean floor.

"Jesus!" Moss shouts.

"I didn't think anyone was home," she says, trying to pick up the clothes now scattered all over the floor, along with my pride. Her eyes stay half-closed.

"Neither did we," Moss says. I can feel my face exploding into dark shades of red.

Moss's mom tries to back out of the room, but her eyes still aren't open all the way, and she runs into a wall. "Please proceed. Pretend I was never here."

Moss stands up and says, "Not likely." He helps me off the bed but doesn't let go of my hand. "We'll leave."

"No! No, please stay. Love each other. There isn't enough love in the world." And now I see why Color loves her mom, because she sounds really nice and genuine. I would never say this to Color, but she sounds just like her.

"It's OK. Esther needs to get home anyway."

Moss's mom looks at me warmly. "Esther . . . Your girlfriend?"

"Not that it's any of your business," Moss clarifies.

Is that what we meant when we said we were "beyond algebros"? My stomach drops a bit at the word "girlfriend." I look at Moss and respond with a simple, happy smile.

"Yes, Esther. We've met once before. With the turkeys." Moss's mom puts the basket of laundry down and comes over to shake my hand. A hand that was just exploring her son's body, intimately. I wave instead.

"Hi, Ms. Jones," I say. "It's nice to see you again."

"Really, you don't have to leave. I'll go." She moves toward the door, but Moss and I get there first, my hand still clasped tightly in his.

"You do that enough," Moss says. "It's my turn." And just like that, the Moss I first met, the boy who keeps his true thoughts inside and makes sharp comments, is back. I feel the sting of his words, but if his mom does, it doesn't register on her face.

"It's good to see you again, Esther."

"You, too."

I don't think I breathe fully until I'm outside of the house and the cooler air hits my skin. We both laugh, and I see Moss relax again. He pulls me back into his chest, the sunset painting his cheeks with an orange glow. I really do need to get home, but then his mouth is on mine and we're kissing, and suddenly time doesn't exist.

And kissing feels OK.

"More than algebros," I say.

"I think we're a bit past that."

Moss kisses me again, but this time it isn't rushed and anxious. I'm not reaching for anything but his lips. We come together in a tangle of tongues and breath.

Moss cradles my face with his cool hands. He leaves them on my cheeks as I pull back, a cloud of warm breath between us. My face hurts from happiness.

"I need to go." I reluctantly grab my bike and notice the garage door is open. The old beat-up station wagon is gone.

"Where'd it go?"

"That thing was a piece of junk. It needed a new life." He knocks up the kickstand on my bike. "Race you home?"

He starts down his driveway as I jump on my bike to take off. Moss runs next to me until we get to my street, and then he has to turn in a different direction. Tom would kill me if he knew I was more than algebros with someone. I can't risk it.

I know I said I wasn't going to lie anymore, but the more I try, the more it just seems inevitable. Especially when it comes to love.

∞

The pool is cold tonight. I'm wrapped in a blanket, holding the only picture I have of Amit and me.

"Are you mad?" I ask him. He just keeps smiling.

"Have you moved on, too?" Amit's happiness isn't helping.

I inhale the cold air. "Is it wrong, what I did today?"

Damn it, Amit. He just keeps looking at me like he loves me. But I can't conjure him next to me anymore. Not even for a second will the past wave over me, so I can imagine touching Amit's cowlick one last time. Lying here in the empty pool, it's only me, even when the wind blows.

I point to myself in the picture. "I gave that shirt away. And those pants." I take another breath and feel tears roll down my cheek. "And you. I gave you away, Amit. I'm sorry. Please don't be mad at me. But I'm not that girl anymore." The tears come faster now. "I gave her away, too. I just didn't want to fight anymore. Are you ever just tired of fighting?"

Amit smiles.

"I know. You're not the fighting type."

I sound crazy right now, talking to a picture, but maybe my words will echo all the way to Ohio, and Amit will know it's OK to move on.

"We can be happy, right? The both of us, even if we're not together?"

Amit just keeps smiling.

"What do you call a number that can't keep still?" I ask him. I wish him to talk. To tell me this is fine. Amit would like Moss . . . eventually. "Come on. You're the one who taught me this joke."

I lie down and look up at the stars.

"A roamin' numeral," I say, hoping Amit hears my joke and laughs.

31

Mom has a brilliant idea, which she declares over a breakfast of scrambled eggs.

"Tom, you should take Esther to work with you," she says.

"What?" he says.

"What?" I say.

"What?" Hannah says.

"I've been reading about experiential education. It's where kids learn outside the home by engaging in real-life opportunities." Mom gestures to Tom. "Tom works at a bank." Mom gestures to me. "Esther, you like numbers. It'll be like a work-study thing. Like what Color does."

I drop my fork. It's the first time Mom has said Color's name in front of Tom. She always just refers to her as "the person from Happy Houses Cleaning Company."

"Color?" Tom asks. "What the heck does that mean?"

Mom goes back to intently making eggs. "One of the girls who comes to clean the house is named Color," she says nonchalantly.

"That's an extremely odd name," Tom says.

His tone reflects his instant judgment. He already doesn't like Color, just based on her name, because with Tom, abnormal is automatically bad. God, why does Tom suck so much?

"Her name isn't the point," Mom says exasperatedly. Her tone reflects that she finds Tom exhausting, and I love her a little more. "The point is that Color does a work-study program through the high school. I thought maybe we could do something similar."

"You're talking about the girl who tried to steal our stuff," Hannah says. "She's a klepto, Tom."

"No, she's not," I say sharply. Hannah is so annoying I can barely stand it. "I told her she could have it. You're a liar, Hannah." All this judging and name-calling has my blood at a boiling point. But oddly, when I call Hannah out on her truth, she goes back to her toast and actually shuts up for once. Satisfaction replaces anger. I knew I was right about her.

"Color is not the focus of this conversation," Mom says. "Esther is."

"Like always," Hannah mumbles, but we all ignore her.

"I'm confused," Tom says. "You want me to take Esther to work with me to teach her about money? What is this—*Mary Poppins?*"

Mom sets a plate of burned bacon down in front of us. "Not to teach her about money, but so Esther can see what you do, so she can engage in math in a real sense. Her math work is so over my head, she's basically teaching herself. She needs adult interaction. Plus, she might want a similar job when she's older."

"Not likely," I whisper. No one seems to hear me.

"She's talented with numbers, Tom. It could be a good fit."

"Well, what do I get to do?" Hannah asks. "I'm talented."

"Not like Esther, honey." Mom pats Hannah on the back. "What do you think, Tom?"

He sits back in his seat and considers it, and I pray he says no. I actually ask God to do something for me. You'd think God would be receptive to my limited requests, since I rarely bother him for miracles and favors.

"OK," he says. "I'll set it up for next week."

"Great!" Mom looks at me, excited. "I think this will be quite an experience."

And I say in my best British accent, "Supercalifragilisticexpialidocious." Thanks a lot, God.

∞

"It turns out there's only one Christian adoption agency in California," Beth whispers. We're supposed to be singing at choir practice. "It's called Christ Connects California."

"So?" I whisper back.

"That's probably who your mom and Tom used to set up the adoption."

Why won't Beth drop this?

"They would have placed the baby with a family," Beth says when I don't respond. Her eyes are intense and bright. The scientist in Beth is coming out. She's a person who likes creating a hypothesis, digging up variables, experimenting with multiple solutions. When you break it down, scientists are really super smart detectives. "They would have the address of the adoptive parents."

"We can't just call the place and ask," I say.

"No. But they would have it in their database."

"A database that's secure, no doubt."

"Nothing is completely secure," Beth says. Shocked, I stare at her as the choir sings and our voices are covered up by three-part harmony.

"What are you saying?"

"I'm saying . . ." Beth leans into me. "There are ways of getting into secure sites."

"Are you talking about hacking?" I ask too loudly. Ms. Sylvia gives me a dead glare as I try to grapple with the fact that Beth just hinted at something illegal. Like really illegal.

"We know who signed the birth certificate and the papers. We know that most likely the baby was placed through this agency. All I have to do is break in . . ."

"Break in"? Did Beth just use those words? She's the one who doesn't lie. Or lies the least. Beth can't start lying for me. "No," I state emphatically. "It's not worth it."

"What? Why not?"

"Because even if we did get the address, I couldn't do anything with it. I'm stuck here."

"But at least you'd have it . . . for someday." Beth looks at me like a girl who's lost something and wishes she could get it back.

"But it'll hurt more than it helps."

"You don't know that. And we're here if it hurts too much. We'll make it better. That's what friends do." Beth takes my hand in hers. "I want to do this for you, Esther. Just think about it."

I think about it and think about it and think about it, but I can't find an answer.

"Do you really know how to hack into things?" I ask.

Beth says in her best Pastor Rick imitation, "Science is *awesome.*"

∞

Kissing Moss is awesome, too. I can't stop. We're hidden from the bike path, off in the tall grass that's shaded by trees, rolling around together like linked tumbleweeds. He's in his perfectly short running shorts.

Moss pulls a piece of grass from my hair and tickles my nose with it. I almost sneeze, and he laughs.

I push him over and roll on top of him. And we're kissing again, and his skin tastes salty. His hand glides under my shirt and up my back. I reach back and unhook my bra, egging him on . . . further. Forget shyness. We're past that.

Moss's hands move to a more reserved position at my lower back. His fingers tickle my skin, but they don't make their way up to my breasts.

"Esther . . ." he says.

"It's OK," I whisper in his ear. I can't keep my hands off him, and I know I should be more standoffish, but he makes it really hard. I blame Moss. He put me on this roller coaster. He's turned me upside down and inside out. He twisted me around until I can no longer see the past when I'm with him. It's like it doesn't exist. I get to be free of it, my view blocked by Moss.

He rolls me onto my back and looks into my eyes. Like really looks, but not in a dreamy way. In an intensely thoughtful way. I try to kiss him again, but he backs away.

"I like you," he says.

"I like you, too." I smile.

The hesitancy painted on Moss's face makes the world tilt a different way, and my stomach drops. The ride can't be over yet. It just started.

"What?" I ask.

"Your life has already been complicated enough by *this*." Moss looks at our intertwined bodies. When he runs his hand over his buzzed head, I sit up, sick to my stomach, grass stuck in my hair. "I don't want to mess it up any more."

"Any more," I say, rehooking my bra. "You think I'm messed up."

"We're all messed up."

"But me more than others. Now I'm damaged, and you don't want to be with me."

"That's not what I'm saying." Moss shakes his head.

"It sure sounds like it is."

He groans, as I see him slide back into his moody self. "I just want to take it slow so you don't make any more mistakes."

I flinch at the word "mistakes." The past comes back so fast and hard, it hurts my chest to breathe. I didn't make a mistake with Amit. I loved him. And we had a baby. Loving him wasn't a mistake. Having sex didn't feel like a mistake. And *she* isn't a mistake. She is a consequence of my stupid actions that, whether right or wrong, felt truthful at the time. A consequence I keep paying for. Mom was right—this will never go away. My past can only hide. It will never disappear.

This stupid town shouldn't be named Truth or Consequences. It should be named Truth *and* Consequences.

Forget my theory about lying. Everyone is still lying, but here's a more important statement—you can't experience truth without paying the consequence.

It is unavoidable. *That* is why people lie. They lie for love, and they lie because in most cases, the truth hurts more.

I back away from him. "I have to go."

I'm on my bike, faster than ever, riding away from the shaded grass, which still carries the impression of two bodies that for a moment tried to become one. The worst part—I know Moss is fast enough to catch me, but he chooses not to.

32

The truth is that Tom is never going to fill our pool. The truth is that Mom married Tom so she wouldn't have to be a parent all alone. The truth is that Hannah is lying about something. The truth is that Moss just stepped on my heart. The truth is that I hate the cactus outside my window. I've tried to like it. But now, I'm over it.

It's time to cut the damn thing down. I'm sick of looking at it. I'm sick of waiting for it to be something other than what it is—pointy and hurtful. I get gigantic shears from the garage and start hacking away at it.

Mom finds me in the backyard, sweating and grunting. "What are you doing?"

"Cutting this down."

"Why?"

"Because it's hoarding all the water." And I'm out of breath.

"It's a cactus. That's what it's supposed to do, Esther."

"Well, it's selfish. What about everything else that needs water?"

"You can't just go around chopping things down," Mom says. "It looks bad."

I stop and wipe the sweat from my forehead. "Is that why you married Tom?"

"What?"

"Because it looked bad for you to have two kids and no husband."

"Esther, where is this coming from?"

I throw my hands up in the air. "That's why we moved here, right? Because it looked bad that I had a baby. That's exactly why you want me riding my bike all the time, so I *don't* look bad anymore. Why are we so concerned about how we look to other people? It's all a bunch of lies anyway."

"Esther, calm down." Mom tries to take the clippers from my hand, but I pull back.

"You told me this would all go away." I point the clippers at her. "But even that was a lie."

I go back to hacking at the cactus. Mom stands there for a moment, speechless, and then says, "Make sure to clean up before dinner. We're having tacos."

When I'm done chopping the cactus down, I tie some of the string around it and drag it to the front of the house. Our neighbor comes out and watches, clearly intrigued by my erratic behavior, but I don't care. He can watch my meltdown. At least it's honest.

"Be careful. Those things can really hurt you," he says from his porch. "The sting lasts a long time."

"Finally, someone who speaks the truth," I holler back. The cactus finds its final resting place at the end of the driveway. Good riddance.

When Tom gets home and asks me why I cut it down, I say, "Because I needed to."

"You needed to."

"Yes."

"I thought we talked about impulsive decisions, Esther."

"Getting a tattoo seems a little impulsive." I stare him down. Then I tell him I'm sorry, but once a cactus is cut down, it can't be replanted. "I guess I'll have to live with it. But contrary to what you think, it's easier than living without it."

I get up from the table, not hungry anyway.

From my bedroom, I hear Hannah in the kitchen, her theatrical voice piercing. "She's doing it again. She's going to ruin everything."

"Stop being dramatic," Mom says.

"Just wait," Hannah says. "This isn't over."

∞

My nightmare returns. I wake up and hear a baby crying. It's just down the hallway. I'm certain of it. I even get out of bed. But after I search the whole house, nothing. I shouldn't be surprised. It's been empty from the start.

∞

My hair is longer than it was when we first moved. My body is slimmer, not that I was trying to lose weight. I was chasing a boy, and it just happened.

Glaring at my own reflection in the mirror, I examine my brown eyes—my dad's eyes—and see what Moss sees. I'm damaged, broken, and it makes me want to break things so I don't feel so alone.

Here's my problem, and it makes me the worst person on the planet—I tell myself that things just happen. But I make them happen. I break them. *I* am the problem. I am the life-sucking, water-depleting cactus.

"I just want to take it slow so you don't make any more mistakes." Moss's words echo in my head and crush me all over again, because he's right. I make mistakes. That's what I do. I tried not to lie and couldn't do it. I promised my family we'd start over again in Truth or Consequences, and I'm back where I started—messing around with a boy behind the backs of Mom and Tom. And the worst part is . . . I want to do it. I want Moss. It's like the farther I run from myself, the more I just find I'm running in a circle.

The baby I had may not be a mistake, but I'm not innocent.

I turn away from the mirror, unable to look at myself, and squat in front of my fishbowl.

"Even you," I say. "I haven't set you free because I'm selfish and I'm not ready to. I need you. Like I needed Amit. Like I need Moss."

But what if I've ruined her, too? What if my mistakes cost her the freedom she deserves?

Color pushes my door open with her vacuum. Based on the pity all over her face, I know she's talked to Moss. I flop onto my bed, putting the pillow over my head. The white noise of the vacuum isn't loud enough to drown out my shame.

My wallowing only lasts a few moments before Color pulls the pillow from my head and says, "I'm sorry I still haven't found a bigger vacuum to suck up all your problems."

"I'd just ruin it anyway. That's what I do. I'm a prickly cactus. Don't come too close. I'll damage you."

Color sits next to me and pats her lap, signaling me to lay my head on her legs. I do, looking up at my friend.

"Everything and everyone is already broken anyway," she says. "You can't change that."

"But *I* break it. It's my fault."

"So what? You just need some proverbial superglue in your life." Color plays with my hair, her fingers light on my scalp. It's deeply soothing. "You put the pieces back together. It will never be how it was, and it doesn't make it any less broken, but it's new. People can be whole and broken at the same time, Esther."

I recall, *.9 recurring is equal to 1*. Tiny pieces equal the whole.

"Where do I get the superglue?" I ask.

"The hardware store. Duh." Color nudges me.

Her charm works for a moment, but it's fleeting. "I just feel . . . lost."

"Look, Esther, going back to the beginning is impossible. There is no beginning and no end. What was never born can never die. The present is the only place."

"We're approaching the rabbit hole, Color."

She laughs. "All I'm saying is you can't do anything about the past. But it doesn't really exist. Memories are just a mind manipulation to keep you tethered to something that's no longer there. Free yourself and let it go."

I am so tired of holding my pieces together. I need the superglue. But it's not that easy. If I let go of the past, that means I actually have to loosen my grip on *all* of it. "It's a lot harder than it sounds."

"It's the hardest thing you'll ever do."

We let the vacuum run as we sit on my bed, trying to let go of the past. It's so much a part of me that the line is blurred, and I can't see where I need to cut myself free. At what moment?

Eventually she says, "I think something is going on with Jesús. He hasn't been at school or work the past two days, and he's not returning my texts."

"What?" I sit up. I haven't been to HuggaMug to see him because I can't bring myself to look at Moss.

"It's not like him to just completely drop off."

"Maybe he's sick?"

"Maybe." Color doesn't sound convinced. "But I don't think so."

"Well, what does your intuition say?" I ask.

"My intuition says something is going on."

"Can you go to his house and check on him?" I ask.

Color shakes her head. "He yelled at me the one time I stopped by unannounced."

"Jesús yelled? I don't believe it."

"Believe it," Color says emphatically. "I think he's embarrassed. He lives in the trailer park, over on San Pedro Loop. His is the blue one. He's kind of sensitive about it. You know Jesús. He's all about flair. His house doesn't live up to his personality. Like I care about his house. It's his soul I love."

"I love his soul, too."

Then Color lights up and says, "*You* could go check on him. Maybe ride your bike past and drop in?" She grabs my hand. "I just need to know that he's OK. If he's sick, we can help him. Bring over some chicken soup or something."

Now that Color's brought it up, it would feel good to *help* someone for a change. To stop destroying everything. I need to stop sulking.

"Of course, I'll do it," I say.

"Thank you." When Color pulls back from the hug she's enveloped me in, she has a mischievous furrow to her brow. "My intuition tells me everything is going to be OK with you and Moss."

"Really?" My heart doesn't feel so convinced. It hurts in a broken way.

"Really."

"I think I'm gonna need a lot of superglue for this one."

"Don't we all," Color says. "By the way, your Christmas gift is almost done." Then she's back to vacuuming.

"You really didn't need to get me anything."

But at that moment, she opens the closet door and screeches, her surprised gaze moving between me and the items in my closet, or lack thereof. "It's empty. I can't believe it's empty. You did it, Esther. You got rid of all your boxes."

I lift up the bed skirt to show her a few lingering ones still stuffed under my bed. "Almost."

"Well, at least the closet is empty. That's progress. Have you named the fish yet?"

"I have an idea, but I don't know . . ."

"Whenever you decide, you have to tell me," she demands.

"You'll be the first to know."

Color vacuums the carpet in my closet with happy vigor, then says, "Can you come over Friday and get your gift?"

"I'm going to work with Tom during the day." I fake gag myself. "But I should be able to ride over after."

"And don't forget about Jesús."

"I could never forget about him."

"Bring some superglue. Jesús might need it."

The smile never fades from Color's face as she pushes the vacuum out of my bedroom and closes the door behind her.

33

I wake up two days later and smell it. Rain.

But it's a sunny Thursday, and as the day wears on, I ride my bike through the HuggaMug drive-through looking for Jesús. No clouds. I must have imagined the smell. I don't really want to be here, but I also really want to find Jesús, so I put my bruised ego aside and yell, "Beep!" Plus, I've had such a hard time sleeping the past few days, I need coffee. Lots and lots of coffee.

Moss sticks his head out of the drive-through window, forcing my stomach to splat all over the ground. I don't even bother picking up the pieces. I need superglue. Pronto.

"Hey," he says.

"Hey." My eyes are on my feet. "Is Jesús here?"

"He didn't show up. Again." Moss acts annoyed, so I act annoyed at his annoyance.

"OK." I turn to ride away.

"Esther, wait." Moss closes the drive-through window and comes out of the coffee shack.

"What?" I snap.

"Can we talk?"

"About what?"

"You know what."

"OK." I put the kickstand down on my bike. I say "OK" like I'm not really OK with any of this, and Moss knows it.

"I'm sorry," he says.

"About what?" My sarcasm is getting out of control.

"You know what." Now it's Moss's turn to look down at his feet. He's wearing his running shoes and shorts. It's a little chilly for shorts today, but the sun makes it better. He's probably going for a jog after work, along the path. Our path. My throat gets tight and tears threaten. I want to ride with him. Next to him. Be with him. But sorry isn't enough. I want more than sorry. I want forgiveness for being me. But I'm not sure Moss can give that to me.

"Forget it." I move to get back on my bike, but Moss grabs my arm.

"I've never had sex before."

Now, I'm sorry—*what?!*

Moss can't look at me. "I got nervous. Because I don't want to mess this up."

"Oh," I say.

"And I don't want you to feel like you *have* to do it. I'm not in any hurry. But I don't care if you're damaged. I like your damage—it makes you . . . you. And I like *you*."

He's still holding my arm, so I take it as an invitation to step closer. My freezing attitude is melting in the sun.

"I like your damage, too," I say.

"I don't know. I'm pretty damaged." Moss rubs his head, his habit's familiar, just the way I like it. Just the way I like *him*. "I just want you to trust me. Do you trust me?"

"I trust you." The words come quick, unfettered. "Do you trust me?"

Moss nods, and just like that, we're back to kissing. He wraps his arms around my waist and holds me closely. I think I could stay here forever. Tangled in damaged and broken parts, but locked in trust.

But Jesús is waiting . . . And he needs me. When I peel away from Moss, it feels like Velcro that doesn't want to separate, but the sun is hanging lower in the sky, and my time is limited. I'll need to be home soon.

"I need to check on Jesús."

"Right now?" Moss licks his lips. Holy sweet Jesus, I want to stay, but . . . Jesús.

"I'll be quick, and then I'll come back."

"I'll be here until we close at five thirty."

"Five thirty," I say.

I get on my bike, and Moss stops me. "Tell Jesús to get his ass back to work." And then Moss adds, "Also, I miss him."

At San Pedro Loop, in front of the only blue trailer in the park, I rest my bike on the gravel, prepared to check on Jesús and get back to Moss before HuggaMug closes. But I should know better than to expect the expected.

∞

"What do you want?"

The woman who lives in the blue trailer is not what I envisioned at all. She's rail skinny, her jeans hanging off her body, and she's smoking a cigarette, which is kind of French, like Jesús, but she carelessly flicks ash on the carpet, like it doesn't matter if she burns down the trailer. Jesús would never be that thoughtless.

"Is Jesús here?"

With a long drag of her cigarette and a tap, ashes rain onto the ground at her feet.

"Is this a joke or something?" she says.

Good question. I'd like to know the answer to that myself.

"No. Is he here?"

The woman puts her cigarette out by rubbing it dead on the screen door. "Jesús hasn't lived here in months."

"I'm sorry. What?"

She points a really bony finger in my face and says, "And you can tell that faggot that he's not welcome back here. Not until he stops his disgusting, filthy ways. It ain't right. I won't have that in my house."

"But he's your son," I say.

"And?"

"And . . . you're supposed to love him?"

"Love?" She spits the word at me. "I ain't gotta love nobody. Especially someone like him."

If Jesús hasn't been living here, where is he?

The need to leave overwhelms me. Without a goodbye or a look back at the woman who's supposed to love Jesús unconditionally, I ride away. I hope I never go back there. I hope Jesús doesn't either. That place is death on earth.

The strangest thing happens as I ride away from that hellhole—I realize that I love Mom and Tom a little more for moving us to the desert. It could have been a lot worse.

∞

I make it back to the HuggaMug after the sun has completely gone down and the streetlights are on in town. I don't know what time it is. The neon **OPEN** sign is off, but a light inside the shed is still on. Hopefully Moss is still here. And while making out with him right now sounds delicious, we have bigger problems. Where is Jesús, and where has he been living?

I bang on the HuggaMug door.

"Moss, open up! We need to talk!" More banging. More pounding. "It's about Jesús! Come on, open up!"

My hand starts to hurt from the pounding, but my pain means nothing. Then I notice a red ten-speed bike.

And the door opens.

"What about Jesús?"

It isn't Moss. It's Jesús.

∞

I throw my arms around him when he opens the door.

"Mon chéri," he says into my neck, like this isn't a big moment at all.

I shove him in the chest. "What the hell is going on?"

Jesús can't look at me, and that's when I notice that his usual clean, groomed self is disheveled. His perfectly waved hair is messy. I want to take back the shove, so I grab his hands and say in the softest voice ever, "What is going on?"

We sit on the couch—a couch that I've sat on numerous times. A couch that's there for hanging out while he and Moss work their shift. A couch that we talked about truth on. A couch that is presently set up to be a bed.

Here is a notable thing about Jesús. He hasn't been living in the trailer on San Pedro Loop. He's been living at the HuggaMug.

"Welcome to my home, mon chéri." Jesús makes a grand gesture. "It's not much, but it's better than where I was living."

After having met his mom, I have to agree.

"Start at the beginning," I say.

Jesús sits back on the couch, closes his eyes, and spills his truth all over the HuggaMug floor.

"My truth is that I'm homeless."

But he says he can't write that for his senior statement, or the school will call the cops. Truth . . . and consequences.

∞

It was a love letter written months ago with red hearts on pink paper, all pasted together. Jesús folded it up and left it in his room.

> Brett—
> *I miss soccer season and your shorts. And the way you kick the balls in your shorts. Throw a guy a bone?*
> *All my love, Jesús*

He never planned to give it to Brett. He wanted to hang it in Heaven. His mom found it before he could. The love letter was thrown in the garbage, and Jesús was thrown out of the house.

Jesús has been living at the HuggaMug ever since. When I ask him why he didn't tell us, he says it's because he was embarrassed. It was bad enough to live in a trailer, but to live with parents who hated him, when we were all surrounded by parents who at least accepted us for who we are, was too much. I tell Jesús that's only partly true. My parents are hiding my past from everyone, especially people at church, and if the secret ever gets out, who knows what will happen. I might need to move into the HuggaMug with him.

Jesús laughs a little bit.

When I ask him why he hasn't been at school, he tells me that he's been showering at the campground just north of town, along the Rio Grande where they have public showers and bathrooms, until a few days ago when it went under remodeling.

"I can't go to school like this." Jesús gestures to his wrinkled clothes and messy hair. "They'll figure it out, and I can't go home."

He fiddles with his hands in his lap. I want to hold him and never let go, but the sun has completely set, and I'm late.

"Why didn't you at least tell Moss and Color? You could stay with them."

"Everyone has their own problems. I don't want to be a burden." And there is the real truth—Jesús is the person who always helps but doesn't want to be helped. "I'll figure it out. I just need a few days," he says. "Please don't tell anyone."

And how can I say no? Jesús is finally asking for something, so I say, "OK. But I'm here if you need me. You know where I live."

"And you now know where I live," Jesús says, and it breaks my heart.

I leave him at the HuggaMug alone, and tell him that he has a few days to sort this out before something needs to happen.

Tom asks why I'm late for dinner, and Mom says I must have had an extra good workout because I'm sweating like crazy, and Hannah isn't home because she's at church practicing with the special choir, and I've never been more thankful for our empty home with a pool that might someday be filled with water.

34

Tom's job at Bank of the Southwest is super boring, and so is his office.

"This is my computer."

Duh. I've seen one of those before, even if Mom and Tom have strict rules about how much I'm actually allowed to use one.

"And these are my cards."

Tom has business cards with his picture on them. He's smiling, but it looks forced.

He exhales like he's super uncomfortable. "And this is my chair."

"Can I sit in it?"

"Sure."

I sit in the chair. This is going to be a really long day. And all I can think about is Jesús. Did he show up for school today? How is he feeling? Does he need me? I stare at Tom's stapler. How do I hold it together when Jesús is falling apart?

"Esther." Tom says my name loudly.

"Huh?"

"I'm telling you what I do, and you're staring at my stapler."

"It's a nice stapler."

Tom ignores the comment and goes on to tell me about opening up bank accounts, how some people want to invest in CDs, how interest accumulates when the bank reinvests the money that people invest in the bank, and then each person gets a sliver of the return on their investment.

But I can't get invested in this conversation. I have too much on my mind.

Tom is exhausted with me by ten in the morning. "Seeing as you like the stapler so much, why don't I find something for you to staple?"

Since I'm relegated to an empty office room with Tom's business cards and a stack of pamphlets about "wise investments," my job today is to staple the cards to the pamphlets. I'm sure this is just what Mom envisioned when she suggested this ludicrous idea.

We eat lunch at his desk. Mom packed us tuna salad. After lunch, the tuna smell lingers, and I go back to stapling.

Sometime in the afternoon, Tom interrupts my stapling, a job that has actually become slightly meditative. Mom's idea wasn't so bad, and while I don't want to do this again, Tom and I have gotten along better than I thought we would. I feared Tom would be all over me, but he's surprised me. Turns out, we both appreciate avoiding the other.

"We have a client here who wants to discuss investment options for a large sum of money she's just received," he says. "Why don't you sit in on the meeting with me?"

And since Tom has actually been kind of cool today, and I've enjoyed the mind-numbing task of stapling, I decide to say, "Sounds great."

We head back through the bank to another unused office. When the door opens, though, my meditative, sedate world ignites.

The events that occur are somewhat blurry in my head, but go as follows.

Tom says, "Mrs. Jones, it's good to see you."

She says, "It isn't Mrs. It's Ms. I'm not married."

Tom says, "I'm sorry about that." I think he really means he's sorry she's not married because all good women need to get married. But I know this woman, and there is no way she could commit to a man. She can't even commit to her kids.

Color and Moss's mom says, "Esther! It's so good to see you. What are you doing here?"

The conversation falls apart from there.

Tom: How do you know my daughter?

Ms. Jones: Because she's dating my son, Moss.

Tom: You have a son named Moss?

Ms. Jones: And a daughter named Color.

Tom: Color?

Ms. Jones: The world just needed more color, so that's why I named her Color.

Tom (looking at me): The girl who cleans our house?

Ms. Jones: She's part of a school program.

Tom (still staring at me): I'm sorry. Did you say my daughter is dating your son?

Ms. Jones: My son, Moss. (With her hand to her face, like she's telling Tom a secret.) I caught them the other day, if you know what I mean. She winks.

Tom: Moss.

Time is moving so slowly, and my brain catches up only enough to say, "But I'm not your daughter."

It turns out the large sum of money Ms. Jones wants to invest is from her recent sale of a Blockbuster.

∞

I try to plead with Tom. I wish I could say this is the first time in my teenage life that I've begged for understanding, but I had a baby out of wedlock, which is cause for much begging and pleading. But Tom doesn't understand that love is love is love is love is lying.

Tom's sleeves are rolled up, exposing his snake tattoo because he's so hot with anger. "You want answers, Esther," he says. "Why don't you start with the problem? *You* are the problem in this family. *You.*"

I've reduced Tom to expose and utter his truth. Again.

He was the one who took control of the situation when I told them about the baby. Outside, the wind blew the rest of the autumn leaves all over the driveway. It was raining.

"You're what?" Mom asked.

"I'm pregnant."

"I don't understand how this happened," Tom said.

"The usual way," I said.

"Don't be smart with me."

"Didn't I raise you right?" Mom talked to the air, not me.

"I'm sorry," I said.

"You're sorry?" Tom said. "Sorry doesn't mean much right now. How could you do this?"

"I'm sorry." It was the only thing I could think to say.

"Sorry doesn't erase the problem," Tom said. He used that word—"problem." You can't erase problems. You solve them. "Sorry doesn't erase bad choices. You were supposed to give yourself to Christ, not some teenage boy."

"This is my fault. You had no father for too long," Mom said.

"Don't worry, Julie, I can fix this," Tom said, touching her leg. "We'll take Esther out of school. We'll wait out the pregnancy here, and when it's all over, we'll move. No one needs to know."

Tom got in my face then. "Tell me the name of the boy."

And with the same force Tom had applied, I pushed back, just this once. "No."

But secrets always come out.

After the scene at the bank with Tom and Moss's mom, I'm grounded for life. This time I don't bother saying sorry.

Supercalifragilisticexpialidocious.

∞

Tom puts my bike on the lawn with a **For Sale** sign. Just like Heaven. Soon the bike will be gone, too.

Complex Math Problem: What is the cost of innocence?

The answer doesn't matter. Later that day, someone steals the bike and leaves the **For Sale** sign behind.

∞

I don't make it to Color's on Friday to get my Christmas present. I'm being held captive. On Saturday, I rearrange the glow-in-the-dark stars on my ceiling to look like actual constellations. That's how bored I am.

Hannah comes into my room dressed up like she's going out—tight jeans, boots, and a shirt that's probably too tight, but Mom and Tom are so focused on me right now, they don't notice Hannah. She's also clutching her Bible. I am so done with that thing I want to scream.

"You have a boyfriend?" she asks in a tone that's not nice at all.

I jump on my bed, putting the final stars in the ladle of the Big Dipper.

"How do *you* have a boyfriend?"

"Just go away, Hannah."

But she doesn't. Hannah stands there like she wants to say something but can't actually get the words out. I complete the constellation. Then I stand staring at Hannah as she fumbles with her words. Her annoying factor is through the roof right now because my patience is thin. I am living in a house of lies, and yet I'm the only one who ever gets busted.

"What do you want?" I bark at her.

Tears collect in Hannah's slightly surprised eyes, and she points the Bible right at me.

"Why does everyone always fall in love with *you*?" Hannah turns, whipping her hair over her shoulder, and storms out of my room, slamming the door. A lonely star falls from my ceiling and lands on the bed. I marinate in Hannah's words and ask my fish if my relationship with Hannah will ever be repaired.

Even my fish shakes her head. No.

∞

Mom reacts a bit differently to the news that I have a boyfriend named Moss. It's Monday and the doctor's office is busy. The magazine pile hasn't changed from the last time I was here. Mom leans down, picks up a magazine, and then puts it back.

"Magazines are the most toxic things in a doctor's office." She sits forward, her elbows on her knees. "Everyone picks them up while they're waiting and gets their germs on the pages."

But Mom always has hand sanitizer, which she promptly pulls from her purse and applies to her fingers. She squirts some in my palm.

"Thanks," I say.

She sits back in the seat and looks at the door.

"Don't ever tell Tom I did this."

"OK."

"He doesn't understand. Men don't understand. They can't. It's women who carry the burden. Men walk away unscathed." Mom shakes her head. "I'm doing this because I care. I won't have your life ruined."

"OK."

"And we will never talk about it again." Mom reaches out for the magazines once more and stops. "I almost forgot."

"Germs," I say.

Mom looks at me. "Do you like Tom? Don't answer that." Her bouncing feet shake our seats. "He's a good man. A good man, but he isn't perfect. Perfect is overrated."

"That's what Color says."

"I've always liked her. Smart girl." Mom's smile fades. "You'll understand when you're older, Esther, why we do all of this."

"OK."

"Stop saying 'OK.'"

"OK." I glance down at the magazines. "Sorry."

"Don't say 'sorry' either. Women apologize too much. Men don't do that." She puts on another layer of hand sanitizer. "Just in case," she says.

We sit in silence as we wait for my name to be called. Then Mom says, "I spy with my little eye . . . something blue."

"Is it me?" I say sarcastically. Mom doesn't appreciate it. "Just kidding."

We play the "I spy" game, like I'm seven years old and sitting in the pediatrician's office, instead of sixteen years old and waiting for my gynecologist to put me on birth control.

∞

My head is stuffed in the pillow when I hear a tap on the window. I had the dream again—crying and crying and no way out—and the pillow isn't really helping. I look out into the yard where the cactus used to be, but I see nothing. Rearranging the pillow, I lie back down. The only lights on in the house are the stars on my ceiling.

Another tap comes from the side of the house. I sit back up, pausing before deciding to crack open the window as quietly as possible. Cool air flows in.

"Esther?"

"Jesús?" I find him huddled against the house in the dark. "What are you doing?"

"Can't a guy come see a girl in the middle of the night? Most people would find this moment romantic. It's very Romeo and Juliet of me."

"They kill themselves in the end. There's nothing romantic about it. And you're gay."

"Maybe Romeo was gay and he just didn't want to admit it."

"Mercutio is gay."

"He is?"

"Yes. He's in love with Romeo."

"Wow. Consider my mind blown."

"Stop dodging my question. What's going on?" I ask.

Jesús comes right up to the window, his face tired and dirty.

"You said I knew where you lived if I needed you." He grabs my hands. "I need you."

And I say what Jesús says to every customer who drives through HuggaMug. "Let me help you."

"You can start by telling me something beautiful." Jesús presses my hands to his cheek. "Tell me what it feels like to be in love."

To put that into words is so hard, but I swim through my memories of Amit, searching for the right piece for Jesús.

"Amit told me about a woman in India named Amma. She sits in this temple all day, and people come from all over the world to see her."

"Why?"

"So she can hug them."

"Why does she hug people, Esther?" Jesús whispers.

Here is a notable thing about love. I've realized it isn't as complex as people make it out to be.

"Because people don't understand that love is that simple," I say.

"You've felt love that simple?"

With my hand pressed to Jesús's cheek, I change my theory. Maybe love isn't lying. Maybe people just like to complicate things.

Because the truth is that the best kind of love is simple.

But because we're not perfect humans, we mess it up.

"Yes," I say.

"Why can't my parents love me like that?"

"Because some people only see the ugly in life." My hand moves to cup his cheek.

"Am I ugly?"

"No. You are beautiful."

"I don't feel beautiful," he says. "I want to know simple love."

After quickly closing my bedroom door, I open the window wide enough for Jesús to climb in. He stands right in front of me, and we see each other through the darkness. But the shadows mix with the night and fade away. I move in close, wrap my arms around him, and press myself into Jesús, like air fills the lungs. I cling to every piece of him as we stand in my room, hugging.

"Can you feel it?" I say in his ear.

His face rests on my shoulder. He breathes warm air onto my skin. The weight of what he's carrying is palpable, but the longer we hold each other, the more I take from him. Jesús relaxes and says, "Yes."

I won't let him go back to the HuggaMug. Instead, I hide him in my clean closet. I knew getting rid of that baggage would be good for something.

∞

We talk in whispers. The closet door is shut.

"Do you smell that?"

"What?" Jesús asks.

"Rain," I say.

"I didn't see rain in the forecast." Jesús talks into my neck, his face close to mine.

"I can smell it." I turn so our noses almost touch. "Do you think it's raining in California?"

"Maybe."

"Jesús?"

"Yeah, Esther?"

"I'm grounded forever because Mom and Tom found out about Moss."

Jesús says, "It's the pits."

"Yeah. The pits." A pause lingers between us. "Jesús?"

"Yeah, Esther?"

"Since I'm already grounded forever, things can't get much worse, right?"

"You're talking to a homeless teenager. It can get worse."

"But you wouldn't go home, even if your parents offered to take you back, right?"

Jesús thinks for a moment. "No. I wouldn't go back. I have more respect for myself than that."

"In a way, you're free, then."

Another second passes. "Yeah, I guess so."

I roll onto my back and look up at the closet ceiling. Jesús does the same.

"Jesús?"

"Yeah, Esther?"

"I'm in captivity," I say.

Jesús doesn't say anything—I think because he knows I'm right and doesn't want to rub it in.

"Sometimes it has to get worse before it gets better," I say.

"That's probably true."

"You can't stay in my closet forever. You have to tell Moss and Color the truth."

"I know."

We lie in silence and the truth for a while. "Jesús?"

"Yeah, Esther?"

"I think I want to make things worse." I tell him I want to go to California and see the baby. And Jesús says he's glad I'm done making excuses, and that he's been keeping another secret for a while now, too. It turns out Color is giving me the best Christmas gift I could ever ask for—a newly remodeled station wagon, paid for with the profits of a garage sale held on New Year's Day at an old, run-down Blockbuster.

35

Jesús tells Moss and Color the truth the very next day. That night they sneak over to Jesús's old trailer and break three cartons of eggs on the outside. Color and Moss's mom says that since Jesús is eighteen, legally an adult, he can live with them. She's leaving again anyway. There's a farm in Portland where she can spend the next few months trimming weed and making over ten thousand dollars.

Jesús tells me all of this as we lie on my bed in the middle of the night, looking up at the fake galaxy above.

"Did you tell them I'm grounded for infinity?"

"Yes, but Color wanted me to tell you not to worry. She's got a plan."

"I miss everyone," I say. I know it's been less than a week, but I do.

"Fungus misses you, too." Jesús nudges me. "I'm so jealous. You get to make out. What's it like kissing someone?"

I look at Jesús. "You've kissed someone."

"Not for real, I haven't." He looks at me like *duh*. "Gay boy in a small town. The odds are not in my favor. There isn't another gay kid for miles."

Except for Beth, but she hasn't told Jesús yet, and that's not my truth to share.

Just the thought of kissing Moss makes butterflies threaten to explode in my stomach. "It's wonderful."

"Wonderful sounds . . . wonderful," Jesús says, breathless.

"Jesús?"

"Yeah, Esther?"

"You know you're free now," I say.

"I can't believe it took me so long to tell the truth. I could have saved myself months of sleeping on that awful couch in HuggaMug. And the bathrooms at the state park. Yuck." Jesús points at the ceiling. "I see the Big Dipper and Orion's Belt."

"They were easy to replicate."

I wiggle closer to him. Picking up Jesús's hands one at a time, I count all of his fingers.

"Ten fingers. Ten toes. Two eyes. One nose. Perfect."

"What?" he asks.

"Nothing." I wiggle back into the nook of Jesús's arm. He pulls me into his side, snuggling me around the waist. Minutes pass. The night goes on. The fake stars shine above us.

"This is over," I say. "You won't be sneaking in my window anymore?"

"We still have tonight, Esther." Jesús breathes deeply. "And I think you're right about the rain. I can feel it, too."

∞

When I wake up, thick gray clouds that look like waves of condensation hang in the sky. Jesús is gone. I didn't even feel him leave.

Mom looks at me weirdly when I stick my hand out the front door and check for rain, but the air is dry.

"I don't think it's supposed to rain today," she says.

"Maybe the news is wrong."

She pokes her head out the door and looks up. "Those aren't rain clouds."

"How do you know?"

"I lived in Ohio long enough to know the difference."

"Do you miss it?"

Mom wipes her hands together, like she's getting rid of dirt from her fingertips, but nothing is there. "How about grilled cheese for lunch?"

It's amazing how long people will live with their lies, even when the truth will set them free.

36

It doesn't rain for the rest of the week. Clouds cover the sky, but not a drop falls. I guess I was wrong. I was also wrong about my lying days. They are so not over. Jesús is right. Color totally has a plan. And it starts with Beth knocking on my door early Saturday morning.

Tom answers. "Beth? What are you doing here?"

The second I hear her name, I come running for the door. Beth barely has time to get out, "Hi, Mr. Ainsworth, I was wondering—" before I'm standing at Tom's side.

"Hi," I say, smiling.

"Hi." Beth is wearing a T-shirt that I haven't seen before. It says: **Jesus Christ Is the ONLY Man I Need**. I have to control myself, even though I want to burst with hilarity. "I was wondering if you wanted to help me deliver Valentine's Day cookies and decorations to the people at the retirement community." Beth looks at Tom. "It's for church. I offered to help Pastor Rick."

That really does almost make me laugh.

"He's doing some wonderful things with the youth at church, isn't he?" Tom says.

"He totally is." OK, Beth *so* does not sound like herself, and I love it. "It will only take a few hours, and I have my parents' car."

Beth motions over her shoulder to the driveway, where the newly redone station wagon is parked. Holy freaking hell.

"I don't know . . ." Tom shakes his head. "Esther is kind of . . ."

But Mom comes up behind Tom, puts her hand on his shoulder, and says, "I think it's a great idea. Hannah's at church all day rehearsing. We could have the house to ourselves."

Tom tries to counter. "But—"

"She's been cooped up for over a week. She didn't even go to choir practice. Let the girl go." And when Mom says "let the girl go," she says it in a tone that reminds Tom that I'm not his daughter. I'm *her* daughter.

"OK," Tom says.

I can't help but laugh when Beth pulls down the street and out of sight of my house, and Color, Moss, and Jesús pop up in the back of the station wagon.

"I hope you like your Christmas present, Esther," Color says.

We laugh and laugh and laugh.

∞

"Ten fingers. Ten toes. Two eyes. One nose. Perfect." I stared at the hospital wall, unable to move. "Ten fingers. Ten toes. Two eyes. One nose."

Stop counting, Esther. I heard the words in my head.

"I can't," I said to myself out loud.

Problem solved, Esther.

"But the baby wasn't the problem. She was the solution to *my* problem. All I wanted to see was her eyes."

No one heard me talking at the hospital. The nurse wasn't due to check on me for a while.

"Ten fingers. Ten toes. Two eyes. One nose."

I knew the math—she was half me and half Amit, one full person.

"Perfect."

∞

The first thing I do at Color's house is go straight up to Moss's room and kiss him until I can't breathe. His door is barely shut before my mouth is on his and we're playing tonsil hockey.

We fall back on his bed, making out like we've never made out before, hands groping places Moss wouldn't dare go a few weeks ago. He unhooks my bra like he's done it a million times. I unbutton his jeans, and he wiggles out of them faster than I've seen him run. And we're rolling around in his bed, hands all over each other. Grounding never works. The forbidden fruit only gets sweeter.

This is what I wanted, what I was desperate for. I kiss Moss over and over and tell myself I want this. I want this. I want this. I want this.

But the counting won't stop in my head. *Ten fingers. Ten toes. Two eyes. One nose. Perfect.*

Stop it, Esther, I think to myself.

But I can't.

The counting never stops if the problem is never solved. Or if the solution was taken away in the middle of the night, before I could ever see her.

"Wait." I pull back from Moss.

"What?" he says, out of breath.

"This isn't right."

"What isn't right?" Moss's eyes search my face.

"This." I point to the bed. "We shouldn't do this."

"But I thought it's what you wanted?"

Me, too. I thought this was what I wanted, but the truth is—I want Moss. I want a relationship. I don't want to lie to him or make hasty decisions. I don't want the consequences of our actions ruining us forever. I've done that before. I want to trust him, but more importantly—I want him to trust *me.*

"I do want this," I say to him. "But I also want time."

I want Moss to come to my house and meet Mom and Tom. I want Moss to hold my hand without worrying who might see. I want Moss to run with me biking at his side, free of the past because it's all out in the open. Because we trust each other *with* each other. We don't need to hide because we have nothing to be ashamed of. I did that with Amit, and it tainted everything. We were broken long before we ever knew it.

"Time?" Moss says.

"To get this right."

Moss traces my collarbone with his fingertip. "If you insist."

"You're making this hard."

"Don't say the word 'hard.'"

I swat his hand away, and he laughs.

"Just make sure to tell me when time's up, OK?" he says.

"OK." I grab his hand and count his fingers. "Ten fingers. Ten toes. Two eyes. One nose. Perfect." Moss's gray eyes are so beautiful. "My mom used to say that all the time. She'd tuck Hannah and me into bed and count all our body parts, just to make sure we were still whole. We loved it because she always tickled our feet."

We sit there in silence for a while as I fight the memories off. I'm so sick of fighting. I'm tired and worn out. And done. I am so done.

I get up and grab a blue tack from his dresser. "It's high time we added another one to your map."

"What?"

"I'm ready. I want to go to California."

"Now? We're supposed to have you back at your house in a few hours."

Moss chases me downstairs. Color, Jesús, and Beth are sitting in the overgrown grass in the backyard when Moss and I burst outside.

"Done already?" Jesús wiggles his eyebrows at me.

"It's time," I say out of breath.

"For what?" Color says.

I look at Beth. "Is the offer still on the table?" She perks up, knowing exactly what I'm talking about, and gives me an enthusiastic nod.

"What is going *on?*" Jesús says emphatically.

"The journey is coming to an end," I say.

"Does this mean what I think it means?" Color's face lights up.

I say, "We're going to California."

37

OK, so going to California might be a stretch. First, we need an address of where exactly *to* go. That's where Beth's hacking comes into play.

She gets all excited and starts talking in terms I don't understand, since Mom and Tom won't even let me have an email address.

"All I have to do is get into the VPN for Christ Connects California, which requires a log-in, but I can easily obtain that with some social engineering tactics. From there, it should be easy."

We all look at Beth like she's a mad scientist, and I'm pretty sure she is.

"Is that all?" Moss says sarcastically.

"Beth, you are so hot right now," Jesús says. "I can barely control myself."

She turns red. "Just leave this to me. Do you have a computer somewhere?"

"You can use the one in my room," Color offers. We all move to follow Beth like a pack of wolves, but she stops us.

"I prefer to hack in private. You understand." She disappears upstairs then, leaving us to lie back in the grass and wait, sprawled as clouds roll over our heads, blocking the sun.

"I see a giraffe," Color says, pointing at the sky.

Jesús traces a cloud with his finger. "I see a crown."

"There's a car with three wheels," Moss says.

But the clouds shift too quickly for me, and the moment I think I see something, it dissipates into nothing. I'm distracted by the fact that at any moment, Beth might come outside with information that will change my life.

"Can I really do this?" I ask my friends.

Jesús says, "The better question is—Can you not?"

But it turns out that the answer doesn't matter. Beth comes outside a while later. She doesn't look happy.

"I couldn't find it. I got into the VPN and everything, but nothing's a match. I couldn't find a birth certificate or the papers with your mom's name anywhere."

I stand up, but leave my heart on the ground, coated in disappointment. "That's OK. You tried."

"This isn't over, Esther," Beth says. "I can try other adoption networks in California. It's just getting late, and I need to get you home."

"Don't worry," Color says, hugging me. "Trust in Dharma. We'll make it to California somehow."

Beth drops me off in the old station wagon, and Tom asks how it went delivering valentines. I say fine.

And he says, "You don't look fine."

And I say, "I'm just not feeling very well."

"Are you sick?"

"Maybe."

And then Tom makes a cross with his fingers and says, "Stay away from the rest of us, then."

"Not a problem," I say, and disappear into my room for the rest of the day.

∞

The knock at my bedroom window echoes in my head, startling me. Jesús stands out in the darkness, his shoulders shaking. He knocks again and makes a sign for me to open the window.

When I do, I say, "What's going on?"

"I think the rain is coming." Jesús's voice quivers as he glances skyward. "And I thought maybe you needed me." He climbs in the window. "Are you . . . crying?"

"No," I say."

Jesús wipes tears from my cheek.

"OK, yes."

Once he is inside, he pulls me into the closet. "What is it?"

"Why is this so hard?" I whisper, now blubbering like an idiot.

"You're asking a gay boy why life is so hard? I definitely don't have the answer."

That makes me laugh. I wipe tears from my cheeks. "Does it even matter? What if nothing changes when I see her? What if it only makes living harder? What if . . ."

"What if you don't do it at all?"

"Then I'll always wonder." I hiccup with tears.

"Is it harder to wonder or harder to live with it? Whatever *it* is."

Here are a few notable things about Esther. The reason I cut off all my hair when I found out I was pregnant was that I figured maybe Amit wouldn't love me anymore if I changed how I looked. I was wrong. He didn't love me because of my looks, and I knew it, but I hoped anyway. It wasn't the first time. My short hair has now grown out some, and I need a haircut, because I can't be the girl I was when I had long hair and Hannah spent time curling it. I don't want to be. I like how I look *now*. I like short hair. I also have really bad breath in the morning. If I drink orange juice after I brush my teeth, I gag. I love my friends. And some days I wonder whether it might be possible to love Hannah again.

One more notable thing—I think about my dad every day. I wonder if he thinks about me. I think about seeing him again and about the first question I'd ask him.

Do you think about us?

Why did you leave?

Did you not love us?

Was it my fault?

Why?

Why?

Why?

Why?

Wasn't our love strong enough to hold you still?

I know the answer to the last question. I don't want the baby Amit and I created to have the same questions. And if that means I have to live with whatever the consequences are in order to give her that truth, I'll survive it. Even if it makes living harder.

"I'd rather know," I say to Jesús.

He wraps himself around me and pulls me as close as we can get.

"That's my girl." He kisses me on my cheeks. "Mon chéri." He kisses my forehead. Then he stops, his eyes lingering on my lips. The air between us is still and warm and wonderful.

"It's OK. You can kiss me," I say. "I love you."

"I love you, too, Esther," he says.

And so I reach up for Jesús and pull his face down to mine, and we kiss in a real, loving way. It's sweet, but mostly it's simple—the way love should be.

"I'm still gay," he says when our lips part.

"I would never want to change that about you."

Jesús exhales. "Thank God."

∞

I wake up on the floor in my closet and shake Jesús awake.

"What is it?" he asks.

"Ainsworth," I say.

"Ainsworth." Jesús nods but then shakes his head. "I don't get it."

"My last name is Ainsworth."

"Yes it is."

"Beth called Tom 'Mr. Ainsworth.'"

"And?" Jesús asks.

"Hannah and I never changed our last name. It's my dad's name. Tom's last name is Wyatt."

"OK?"

"And so is my mom's," I say. "It's no wonder Beth can't find anything. She's been searching for the wrong name."

38

Mom hands me a banana and my water bottle, examining me thoroughly in the way only a mom can.

"Esther, eat something," she says.

"I don't feel so well." I grab my belly.

Tom makes a cross with his fingers again. "Keep it to yourself."

"I got the part of Mary in the Passion play," Hannah says, like I'm not here. "The virgin, not the slut."

I poke at the banana.

"That's not eating, Esther," Mom says.

Hannah leans her elbows on the table. "Pastor Rick said he'd help me memorize my lines."

"Try some water." Mom pushes a glass toward me. "Hannah, elbows."

But she doesn't remove them. "He said I was the best Mary he'd ever seen."

"Maybe you're dehydrated," Mom says. "I knew it would happen at some point."

"Pastor Rick said I was the prettiest Mary he'd ever seen, too." Hannah is practically yelling.

"I'll be back," I say.

Hannah sits back with a dramatic huff. "Is nobody listening?"

I go into the bathroom and brush my teeth. Then I come back to the table. "Maybe a glass of orange juice?"

Mom smiles like this is a great idea. I take one sip and gag.

Tom stands up rapidly and says, "I can't get sick. I have a big meeting next week. Esther, why don't you stay home from church today."

The plan works like a charm.

And as I watch Mom, Tom, and Hannah pull down the driveway on their way to church, I see a small raindrop fall on the window.

∞

"We have two hours. Three at the most," I say. Color, Moss, Jesús, and Beth assemble on my bed. Beth is typing away on her laptop. When Jesús gets antsy, he goes to the window to watch the rain. It's come on slowly. A few drops here. A few drops there. Now it's starting to pour.

"Those clouds don't look good," he says.

"I'm in," Beth says. We all crowd around her, and she stands up with the laptop. "OK. Maybe I need a private room."

"Try the closet. It's lovely." Jesús opens the door.

Beth declares, "This is the last time I hide in a closet." Then she looks at all of us and says, "I'm gay. You knew that, right?"

And Color says, "Duh."

Moss just kind of shrugs, but Jesús grabs Beth by the arms and says, "Do you know what this means?"

"What?"

"This means I'm not the only one! I mean, I've had my suspicions of other kids, but never actually heard it confirmed."

"We are *so* not the only ones," Beth says.

"Who else do you think?" Jesús asks, intrigued. "No, wait. Let me guess. Leslie Culpepper? Jacques Sweeney?"

"Madeleine Todd?" Beth offers.

"Definitely a potential lesbian," Jesús says. "And there's a sophomore kid. He's for sure gay. I think his name's Paul or Pete or something."

"Can we get back to business here?" Moss says.

"We should start a club," Jesús says to Beth. Then he pats her on the butt and points at the closet. "Now, get in that closet and work some magic."

Before Beth disappears behind closed doors, she looks at me and says, "I'll find it. I promise." And I trust Beth, because she lies the least of anyone I know.

"This is so exciting," Color says, wringing her hands together. "Aren't you excited?"

"I might throw up," I say. Or burst into a million pieces that Color will have to vacuum up next week when she comes to clean . . .

The rain picks up outside.

Beth is doing something totally illegal in my closet, to get information so that I can do something totally illegal, by running off to California as a minor to see a baby I gave up for adoption. I'm pretty sure there are laws against birth moms seeing babies without the consent of the adoptive parents.

> Complex Math Problem: If laws prevent people from
> making dumb decisions, how did we all end up here?

Moss grabs my hand and pulls me down on the bed next to him. "You're doing that thing you always do."

"What?"

"Thinking."

"You do it, too."

We lie down on my bed with an exhale. "Guilty."

I am guilty of having sex with a boy. I am guilty of having a baby. I am guilty of asking too many questions when I should just be satisfied. It's been sunny for four months straight, and all I've wanted is rain. Now it's raining and I still want more. Why am I never satisfied?

The house is just so damn quiet right now.

Jesús knocks on the closet door. "How's it going in there?"

"You can't rush genius!" Beth yells.

Color and Jesús lie on either side of Moss and me, surrendering to the wait.

"The Big Dipper," Color says, pointing at the ceiling.

"Orion's Belt," Moss says.

"I love the stars. They're so humbling," Color says. "It's like the universe's way of reminding us that we are just the teeniest, tiniest pieces of this gigantic, infinite puzzle."

"That's kind of depressing," Jesús says.

"No way," Color says. "It's a puzzle. Without all the pieces, it can't be complete. We are needed."

And in Color's totally odd way of making sense of things, she hands me an answer. I need this piece of my puzzle. Without it, I won't be complete. I won't be whole. I've tried to forget it . . . to forget *her*, but the stars shine every night, even when they're covered in clouds.

And just then, out my window, lightning flashes across the desert.

"One, one thousand. Two, one thousand. Three, one thousand." Color sings the words.

A crack of thunder.

"Three miles away," Moss says. "It's getting closer."

Minutes pass before there's another flash of lightning.

"One, one thousand. Two, one—" Color is cut off by a boom of thunder.

"Damn," Jesús says. "This storm is bad."

Time passes slowly. The cascade of rain on the roof echoes in my hollow house.

"At least your pool won't be empty anymore," Color says.

I can barely hear her over the noise.

"Oh my gosh." The words come from the closet. I swear I hear something else at the same time, but I'm hearing a lot of things right now. Crashing and booming and rain.

"What is it?" Jesús puts his ear to the closet door. "I think she found something."

Lightning strikes again. Color doesn't have time to count. The thunder claps immediately after the lightning strikes. And the house goes dark.

∞

"Oh my gosh." This time the voice doesn't come from the closet. I only know one other person who wouldn't take the Lord's name in vain.

Hannah.

We turn to find her standing in my bedroom doorway, holding her Bible, water dripping from her hair.

At the same time, Beth bursts out of the closet and says, "The internet just went down! Damn it! I almost had the address!"

"What are you doing here?" I ask Hannah.

Her eyes are so wide, they might pop out of her head. "I knew it. I knew I'd catch you doing something. Peter said I was being paranoid, but I was right."

"Peter Marshfield!" Jesús says enthusiastically. "That's the sophomore kid I was thinking of!"

"You aren't sick." It's like all Hannah can see is me, and vice versa. Her eyes bore into me. "What are you doing? What address is Beth talking about?"

"It's not what you think," I say.

"Are you looking for the baby?"

"OK"—I amend my words—"it's exactly what you think."

"I can't believe you're doing this." Hannah comes into the room. She paces, her eyes wild, the Bible clutched in her hand. "You're ruining our lives. *Again.*"

Hannah scans my friends' faces, a look of pure hatred in her eyes. "Why do you love her? Don't you know what she is? What she'll do to you? She'll break your heart! She's so messed up!"

Hannah spreads the truth about me all over the room, painting her pointed words on the walls, like this is Heaven. "She'll only ruin your life! It's not worth it to love her!"

Hannah lifts her hand high in the air, and I think for just a moment that she'll bring it down on me. But instead, she shoves the fishbowl off the dresser, sending it flying. It smashes against the wall. Glass splinters everywhere. Colorful rocks scatter across the floor. Water spills, and my fish flops, struggling for life, as Hannah runs out of the room.

My mind moves slowly, like it's being dragged behind me, bumping against the ground. I pick up a piece of glass, and it cuts my hand. "She shattered it."

"What do we do?" Moss asks, panicked.

The front door slams and Peter's car pulls out of the driveway, but all I can do is stare at my fish on the ground, surrounded by broken pieces.

"I can't believe she hates me this much."

"Esther, what do we do?" Moss is at my side.

I scoop my fish up and hold her in my hands.

"Esther!" Jesús is frantic. Even Color looks scared. And she never looks scared.

My fish sits in my palm, barely moving.

"Get me a cup of water."

"But what about your sister?" Color asks.

I look at her and say, "I promised you and me I'd save this fish, and that's what I plan to do."

When she comes back with a small plastic cup, I drop the fish inside, and we all huddle around to see if she swims.

"Don't float," I say. "Please, don't float."

When my fish starts to flutter, we let out a collective exhale. Then a rumble of thunder rolls through the sky.

"Oh my God," I say. Blood drains from my face. "Hannah."

∞

My fish can't talk. I wish she could. Her world is gone now. I need to apologize for that, but that's what I do to people. Hannah is right. I ruin everything. Now my fish is trapped in a little cup.

All five of us load into the station wagon—a car Color used her hard-earned money to fix for me. I'm *so* not worth it.

Jesús is next to me. "Where do you think your sister went?"

Does it matter? It's over. Hannah will tell Mom and Tom what I was doing. They'll never let me out of their sight. Or worse, Tom will make us move again.

"I'll be this fish." I examine her in the tiny cup. "I've waited so long for this, and look at where I end up."

"Mon chéri." Jesús pulls on my chin so I look at him. "Where do you think your sister went?"

Hannah could be anywhere. Does it matter?

"Why do you love me?" I ask him. Then I pose the question to all of them. "Hannah is right. I ruin everything."

The windshield is covered in rain. Even the rain is ruined.

"Pain is inevitable in life," Color says. "The point isn't to avoid it. The point is to surround yourself with people who catch you when you fall. We're your trampoline, Esther."

And through the rain, a light dawns. It turns out I didn't need to bring that rusty old trampoline from Ohio to New Mexico. I found a new one.

"Church," I say. "Hannah went to church."

∞

Half of the town is experiencing a power outage, but Touchdown Jesus is still lit up. The parking lot is packed with cars.

"What do we do now?" Moss asks as he parks.

I hand Jesús my fish. "Whatever happens, keep her safe. I still need to set her free."

"OK."

"Promise," I say.

"Promise."

And then I ask everyone, "What is a bird's favorite type of math?"

"What?" Beth asks.

"Owl-gebra."

I get out of the car and step in a puddle. Dirt and water run together and make everything messy, but inside the church, it's dry. I can hear the service coming to a close as the congregation collectively sings a hymn.

My feet squish and squeak up and down the hallways as I search for Hannah. I need to stop her before she gets to Mom and Tom.

Lightning and thunder continue to roll through the sky. The choir room is empty, and down in the fellowship hall, the ladies who serve coffee wait for people to filter out from the service, but no Hannah. I get desperate and start pulling open every door. Hannah was always a good hider when we were little and played hide-and-seek. She never made a sound until I'd almost given up, and then she'd peep like a bird to give me a clue.

I stand in front of Pastor Rick's office door. A moment from back at the house comes to me. Did Jesús say Peter is gay? Who actually told Mom and Tom about the special choir group she's been practicing with almost every night? Ms. Sylvia hasn't mentioned it once, even though she's the one who formed the group. And Beth didn't know about it. Hannah's the one who brought it up.

Peep.

The sound of falling rain echoes through the church, like God stored water just for this moment, so he could release heavy drops on the world to weigh us down.

I turn the knob and open the door.

Lightning flashes, and the loudest crack of thunder yet shakes the entire church.

I find Hannah.

With Pastor Rick.

And he's touching her cantaloupes.

39

Pastor Rick pulls his mouth off Hannah's and backs away frantically.

"Esther, what are you doing here?" he asks.

"Do you guys smell fire?" I ask. Hannah wipes her bottom lip and looks at me.

"We were just—" Pastor Rick starts to say.

I cut him off. "She's barely fifteen."

"What?" Pastor Rick looks at Hannah, his face turning white. He doesn't look so gorgeous right now.

"It's not a complex math problem," I say. "Just take this year and subtract it from the date she was born, and you'll get fifteen."

Pastor Rick puts his hands in the air like he's surrendering and glares at Hannah. "You said you were the older sister. You said you were eighteen."

Hannah doesn't look at him. She keeps her whole body aimed at me. "I lied."

"I'm ruined." Pastor Rick paces his office.

"Join the club," I say. "At least this time it's not my fault."

He runs his hands through his not-so-perfectly tousled hair. "If anybody ever finds out . . ."

"Something really is burning," I say again.

"It's me. I'm going to hell. I'm going to be fired. I'm going to be arrested. Oh, God."

"I don't think God can hear you," I say. "The rain is too damn loud."

He grabs my hands. "Please don't tell anyone. It was a mistake. A horrible, terrible mistake. Let's just forget it ever happened."

"Wouldn't that be *awesome?*"

"It would. Please, Esther." He clasps his hands like he's praying to me. *"Please."*

A woman appears in the doorway then, out of breath. It's one of the gossipy women from the front office. Pastor Rick backs up from me, his face almost translucent.

"Rick," she says, trying to get air.

"What is it, Faye?" He wipes his lips with the back of his hand.

"The Lux Mundi." She grabs her chest, heaving. "It's on fire! Jesus is burning to the ground!"

"I told you something was burning," I say.

Pastor Rick shoots me a panicked look and disappears out the office door.

Hannah crosses her arms over her chest. It's the two of us, locked in a room, but it feels more like a boxing ring. "What?"

"How could you?"

"How could I what?"

"You tried to kill my fish," I say. "You broke everything."

"*I* broke everything?" Hannah snaps. She starts pacing the room, running her hands through her hair.

"Why don't you love me?" I ask.

She stops, stone still, and then points at me. "That's your problem, Esther. You're selfish. You're so focused on fixing your own problems, you can't see anyone else's."

"I'm selfish?"

Hannah comes at me. "We moved halfway across the country for you! All to solve *your* problem! We left our home, our friends, our school." She ticks items off on her fingers.

"But I didn't want to leave," I say. "I wanted to stay."

"It's always about what *you* want and what *you* can't have. But you do it all to yourself, and *we* have to pay the price. What about me? What about Mom and Tom? What about what we want? Do you think any of us *wanted* to leave Ohio? But we did it for you, so you wouldn't be ruined. Whenever you get what you want, everything falls apart!"

I feel the earth spinning really fast beneath my feet. Beth said the earth's rotation is actually slowing down, but it feels like the opposite right now. It's pressing on me and swirling the truth into hazy lines of gray.

"I know," I say, grabbing my head.

"And you refused to tell me anything! You didn't tell me you fell in love! You didn't tell me you had sex! You still won't even tell me his name!" Hannah won't stop. She's catching on fire. I have no choice but to let it burn. The room smells like a bonfire, and sirens wail in the background. Her voice quivers, the pain inside her palpable, and as she speaks, I start to break. "When Dad left, you promised you'd always be there for me. It was supposed to be two of us against the world, but you purposefully left me behind. I could have helped you, Esther, but you shut me out."

My head starts to spin. "You're right. You're right about it all."

"I know!" Hannah yells. Then she slumps over. Like she's been carrying a weight all these months. Or maybe, she's been dragging it behind her all the way from Ohio, living in memories that won't stop swallowing her. I'm not the only one tied to the past, unable to let go. Hannah is broken, too.

"I'm sorry, Hannah. I am so sorry."

When Hannah starts crying, she sobs so hard her body shakes and she almost falls to the ground, but I catch her before she does.

"I wanted to love you through all of it," she says, tears wet on her cheeks. "But I wasn't good enough. Why am I not good enough to love?"

Complex Math Problem: Can you subtract love from unconditional love?

"Amit Kahn," I whisper. The surprise in Hannah's eyes breaks my heart even more.

"That's his name?" she asks.

"He's good at math. Almost as good as me. And he has really beautiful eyes."

"Did you love him?"

"Yes," I say. "I loved him."

"Why didn't you let me catch you?" Hannah whispers in my ear. "I would have, Esther. I would have caught you. I wanted to be there for you."

Smoke seeps into the office under the door. I wish there was time for me to answer all of Hannah's questions about the past, but the present is on fire.

"It's smoky, Hannah. We need to leave," I say.

"But what do we do now?" she asks.

"I don't know. I'm all out of solutions."

Hannah covers her mouth with her arm and coughs. Then she grabs her Bible off Pastor Rick's desk and runs her hand over the black cover with gold lettering.

"Esther?" She looks at me, tears on her face. "I may have the answer you're looking for."

40

I'd forgotten the vow Hannah and I made to each other all those years ago. Or maybe I just didn't believe in it strongly enough to remember. Hannah's the one who's been devout. She believes with strength and promises. It may not always be right, but if truth were easy to find, Jesús would have written his senior statement by now.

I should have trusted her.

It's loud and chaotic outside, with fire trucks and police cars and people in their Sunday best.

"Holy hell," Hannah says.

"That's one way to put it."

Struck by lightning, Touchdown Jesus is burning to the ground. The flames are uncontrollable. It's a fire that no amount of water can put out. Touchdown Jesus is slowly disappearing into a pile of wet ash and dust on the front lawn.

Beth, Jesús, Moss, and Color stand in the rain, watching the fire.

"You made it out of church alive!" Color shouts.

"Barely," I say breathlessly. I look at Jesús. "My fish?"

"She's fine."

"You found her." Beth acknowledges Hannah with a nod. "What do we do now?"

Hannah's bottom lip trembles, turning slightly blue. She's always run colder than me. I pose Beth's question to her, as I should have done over a year ago. "I don't know. What do we do now, Hannah?"

It's the question I should have asked before the walls went up and we grew apart. It took me this long to find it.

"I just wanted someone to notice me," Hannah says. "Mom and Tom, they focus on you. But me . . . And then I found someone who took notice." Hannah shakes her head, the rain mixing with her sadness and pooling in a mess on the muddy ground. This is a mess that's going to take a while to clean up, but as if offering somewhere to start, Hannah holds out her Bible to me. "Look inside."

"I don't think—" I start to say.

"Just look inside," she repeats.

So I do.

Here's a notable thing about Hannah. Turns out, she's had the answer all along.

I stare down at the address written on the first page, a California address in Hannah's handwriting.

"Last year, I looked through Mom's drawers and found the adoption paperwork. I wrote it in the one thing I knew Tom would never take away from me."

"A Bible," I say.

"Go see her." Hannah can't look at me.

"What?"

She takes a deep breath, broadening her chest, and transforms herself back into the dramatic teenager I know so well. "If there's one thing Mom and Tom are good at, it's making sure we keep our mouths shut. I have a feeling they won't approve of my behavior with Pastor Rick. Sometimes silence is the best blackmail. I can threaten them with exposing myself if they come after you. That should work for a couple days at least. Long enough for you to go."

"You'd do that for me?"

A flicker of pain crosses her eyes again, but she recovers almost immediately and nods.

"I'm coming with you," Moss says.

Color grabs my hand. "Me, too."

"Me three," Beth says.

"Me four." Jesús holds up the cup. "Plus a fish."

"Hannah?" I say. "Do you really want to do this? Mom and Tom . . . they'll . . ."

But she states firmly, "I finally found a way to get their attention."

The rain continues to fall, Touchdown Jesus won't stop burning, and the station wagon is running. I guess there's only one thing left to do.

"To California," I say.

No one stops us as we drive away. They're too concerned with their own problems to notice mine.

We make a quick stop at my house on our way out of town. I need to get something from my room before we go. I've been holding on to it, and now it's time to let it go.

With the picture of Amit and me in my hand, and pieces of broken glass and rocks all over my bedroom floor, I don't linger. I'll clean that mess up when I get home.

∞

We stop at the border of Truth or Consequences. Moss pulls the car to the side of the road.

"Are you sure you want to do this?" he says.

"Yes," I answer definitively.

"I've always wanted to see the ocean," Moss says.

"To San Diego we go!" Color hollers.

I hold the cup with my fish in it and whisper, "You're almost free." Moss puts the car in drive, and we exit Truth or Consequences.

Somewhere in Arizona, the rain stops. The clouds break, and we watch the sunset in the west as we drive toward the ocean.

41

"My clothes are dry now," I say to Moss. We lie on the hood of the car in the middle of the desert, somewhere deep in Arizona. The stars are bright. Jesús, Color, and Beth are asleep in the station wagon.

"Mine, too," Moss says.

I point to the sky. "The Big Dipper."

Moss points. "Orion's Belt."

"Real stars are so much better than glow-in-the-dark ones," I say. "This is real, isn't it?"

"It sure feels real."

I kiss him, just to make sure.

"Definitely real," Moss says.

"We made it away safely."

I lean my head on Moss's chest, and he says, "For now."

But now is all we have.

And so I'll take it.

∞

Salt water. The smell hangs in the air as I sit on the beach. We made it to California, where the journey ends. It's here that I'll find what I'm looking for. Dharma said so.

Jesús hands me a donut and coffee. Beth and Color walk along the shore, their feet in the ocean.

"It's not an iced soy mocha frap, but it will have to do."

"Thank you," I say.

Jesús squints in the sunlight and I lean into him, like a comfortable piece of furniture, Moss on my other side. The sand is cold beneath us.

"Do you think the water is cold?" I ask.

"I don't know," Moss says. "I'm just trying to wrap my head around the fact that we're here. Another blue tack for the map."

"Well, there's only one way to find out." I stand up, pulling Jesús and Moss to their feet.

"A swim, mon chéri? Only if it's a skinny-dip."

"I will if you will." All three of us wear devious grins.

"I thought you'd never ask," Moss says. He sprints toward the water, taking his clothes off along the way, like a trail of crumbs for me to follow. He dives in headfirst as Color and Beth holler from the shore.

"What are you waiting for?" Moss yells back to us.

It takes one look at Jesús before we're off and running. Beth and Color are next, and soon we're all naked and swimming. It turns out the ocean in California is perfect.

Moss grabs me around the waist and pulls me into him. "Thank you," he says.

"For what?"

"This." He takes a scoopful of salt water and drips it on my head.

"It's like I'm being baptized all over again."

"I bless you, Esther," Moss says, "in the name of . . ." He gets contemplative for a moment before continuing. "Truth, wherever she may be found, and Heaven, which actually exists in a lonely, abandoned Blockbuster. Who knew."

Water runs down my forehead and cheeks. I lick my lips and taste the salt. "Heaven right here on earth."

Jesús swims up to us and takes a scoopful of water, dripping it on Moss's bare head. "Consider yourself baptized, Fungus."

"Do me!" Color hollers, and Beth dips Color's head back in the water so that her hair circles around her head like a red halo.

"My turn," Beth says. Color tilts Beth's head back in the water and kisses her on the lips.

Beth stands back up, shocked. "I added my own flair," Color says.

And just like that, we've all been baptized in the Pacific Ocean, in the name of Truth and Heaven, and I know it doesn't really count, but at this moment, it feels like everything.

It feels like we can go on like this for infinity.

42

A plastic baby swing hangs from the tree in the front yard. I check Hannah's Bible again to make sure the addresses match, even though I know without a doubt that they do.

"Why couldn't the angle get a loan?" I say.

"Why?" Beth asks.

"Because his parents wouldn't cosine."

"I don't get it," Jesús says. "But who cares?"

I count the seconds along with the clock in the station wagon: $60 \times 60 \times 3 = 3,600$.

It's been three hours.

"Why couldn't the number four get into the nightclub?"

"Why?" Jesús says.

"Because he is two square." I can't take my eyes off the swing. It's just so small and innocent.

"What are you going to do when the jokes run out?" Jesús asks.

"Maybe we should just go," I say.

"It's too late now," Moss says.

"Is it?" I look at him. "What if I missed my chance?"

Color says, "Then you'll catch the next one."

Another hour goes by, and now it's lunchtime. The station wagon smells like the potato chips Jesús and Moss are eating. Jesús wipes crumbs from his shirt and leans his head back on the seat. We only stopped in Arizona for a few hours last night to sleep. Fatigue hangs on all of us.

More seconds pass, and then I say, "I only have one more question."

"Is it a joke?" Beth asks.

"No." I pause. "How do you blow up someone's universe?"

Jesús closes his eyes. "Very gently."

An hour later, everyone is asleep but me. Color and Beth are sprawled in the back of the station wagon. Jesús is reclining in the front seat, and Moss is lying in the middle with me, his arm draped over my side. I count everyone's breaths along with the minutes and seconds. They're even, and practically weightless. My breath comes heavy, though, weighted with the anxiety that's clogging my throat.

I close my eyes, needing a break from the swing. The baby probably sits in the seat, without a care, soaring through the air easily, knowing her parent is there to catch her. How it should be.

There's only one more memory left to wash over me before I need to let this go.

"On the count of three, I need you to push, Esther." The doctor's voice echoes in my head. "Are you ready to do this?"

"No!" I screamed. "I'm not ready!"

Everything hurt.

Mom grabbed my hand tightly. "You don't have a choice, baby. You have to do this. On the count of three . . ."

One . . .

Two . . .

"OK, one more joke," I whisper. "What do you call a destroyed angle?" I take a deep breath and step out of the car. "A wrecked angle."

And I pray I didn't ruin her.

Three.

∞

I stand at the door, practicing my speech in my head, but unable to knock.

Hi, my name is Esther, and that's my baby.

Hi, my name is Esther, and that's my baby.

Hi, my name is Esther, and that's my baby.

When the garage door opens, I jump.

A man, dressed in jeans and a white T-shirt, walks out, pushing a stroller.

"Can I help you?" His voice is pleasant and soft, not the voice of a yeller.

"Hi, my name is . . ."

Time passes. Invisible time. How did I get here?

"Actually, I'm lost," I say.

"I can help," he says. "Where are you trying to go?"

"That's a good question," I say. "You have to have a good question to get a good answer."

An object falls out of the stroller and lands on the ground. The man doesn't notice, so I pick it up, biting the inside of my lip so hard it starts to bleed.

"I think someone dropped this."

"Thank you," the man says. "She's not one to keep things inside the stroller. She's a messy little creature."

"Like her mother," I whisper, bending down in front of the stroller and peeling back the shade.

"This is my daughter, Joanna," the man says.

Hi, my name is Esther, and that's my baby.

"Wow," I say. It comes out as a whisper. "She has beautiful golden eyes."

Here's the thing about truth—it can be defined and redefined for eternity. Truth is like infinity. It isn't an answer. It's just an undefined idea that goes on forever. And in this infinite moment, my truth is defined—she is part me and part Amit, but she is *not* my baby. She is her adoptive father's.

I am reminded, .9 recurring is equal to 1.

I set the stuffed rabbit back in the stroller. "Joanna," I say. "Isn't it amazing how there are so many people in the universe—so many people you don't see—and then all of a sudden you see them, and your life will never be the same?" And then I say, "Make sure she's good at math. Girls can be good at math. Way better than boys."

"OK," her dad says with a questioning smile.

"Here." I hand the man the picture of Amit and me. "If she ever wants to know why she has golden eyes."

And I walk away.

I let go.

43

Dharma said that souls have mates. That we don't travel into this life alone. We are connected to people by something that is beyond our knowing. But the soul knows.

"Why don't you let your fish go in the ocean?" Jesús says from the front seat of the car.

"She's a freshwater fish," I say.

I'm sandwiched between Color and Moss. Beth is driving.

"I'm not sure how much longer she can live in that small cup," Color says.

"Don't worry. It's almost over," I say.

"Joanna," Moss says. "I wish Heaven still existed so you could put her name on the wall."

"But she doesn't need Heaven," I say. "She's not lost."

"The first time we met, did you think we'd end up here?" Color asks.

"No way," I say.

"Me neither," Color says. "Another twist in the maze."

Jesús leans toward the sun coming in the window. "I'm gonna miss it here."

"We don't belong in California," I say.

"Where do we belong, Esther?" Moss asks.

And as I breathe, I smell salt water. I found what I was looking for. I just didn't know exactly what it was until today.

I found my soul *mates*.

"Where do we belong?" I repeat the question and lay my head on Moss's shoulder. "Together."

∞

We stand at the edge of the reservoir in Elephant Butte Lake State Park. Our journey is almost over as the sun starts to rise to the east.

"She belongs here," I say. "In New Mexico. I think she always has. I just wasn't ready to let her go."

"Are you ready now?" Color asks.

"Yes." At the water's edge, I hold the cup up to my face and look into my goldfish's eyes. "I think I finally know her name."

"What is it?" Moss asks.

"Esther. Her name is Esther."

I tip the cup into the water. My fish wiggles from her small container and swims away. Free.

My parting words are "And he saith unto them, Follow me, and I will make you fishers of men."

44

The fire at First Community Church of the Covenant Bible Fellowship had burned late into the night. The town of Truth or Consequences watched as Touchdown Jesus crumbled before their eyes. And when the flames were gone and the ash turned to mud, all that was left were two metal rods . . . in the shape of the cross.

∞

Mom and Tom aren't happy. I scared them half to death. Tom says I've made some big mistakes, but so has he, and he's starting to think facing them might be the best place to start. He's wearing a short-sleeved shirt, too. His snake tattoo isn't that scary after all. I remind them that canaries always want to fly, even when they live in cages. It's just natural. Mom says parents want to lock their children up to keep them safe. That's natural, too.

Jesús is happy living with Color and Moss, but every once in a while, he sleeps in my closet—with the door open now. He's still not done with his senior statement, but there's time for that. The truth is always changing.

Pastor Rick disappears. Rumors fly around the church that he ran off and eloped with a young Mexican girl. Young hearts are broken, but Ms. Sylvia is excited to go back to more traditional church songs. A committee meets to decide what to do about the burnt hole and charred metal cross where Touchdown Jesus once stood. Half the people want a new statue. Half the people want to keep it as a reminder. So it just stays as it is. Undefined, with everyone fighting.

Hannah is grounded for a month. One afternoon I ask her if I can curl her hair. She lets me, and we bounce on my bed like it's a trampoline. That night, Moss comes over for dinner with my family.

And the pool . . . Tom says he'll fill it in the spring, when the weather is warmer. I'm inclined to believe him. He bought me a new bike after all.

I stop at the pet store one afternoon on my way to Color's house.

"I haven't seen you in a while," the clerk says. "Back for more fish food?"

"I don't have a fish anymore."

"Don't tell me it got depressed."

"No," I say, watching the canaries in the cage. "She got free."

∞

We sit on the floor in Color's room—Beth, Color, Moss, Jesús, and I—surrounded by family photos. Color took all the ones from Heaven and hung them on her walls.

"OK. We each get one question," Color says, shaking the Magic 8 Ball.

"Just one?" Beth says.

"One." Color is insistent. "OK, me first. Will I ever meet my dad?" She shakes the ball. We look at her, waiting for the answer. "Signs point to yes." With a huge grin plastered to her face, Color passes the ball to Beth.

"Is time travel possible?" Beth asks ardently. Her enthusiasm fades. "Very doubtful."

"My turn." Moss takes the Magic 8 Ball from Beth. "Will I ever go to Antarctica?" He shakes it. "Cannot predict now. This thing sucks." He tosses it in the air to Jesús, who catches it haphazardly.

"Will I ever fall in love?" He spins the ball around in his hands a little too long—worry for what it might say etched on his face. But when he stops and the answer appears, Jesús is joyful. "Yes—definitely."

"The Magic 8 Ball never lies," Color says.

"OK, Esther's turn." Jesús hands it to me. "Pick your question wisely, mon chéri."

I shake the Magic 8 Ball. Just one question? But I have so many.

"Is God real?" I ask. We wait for an answer to appear.

Ask again later.

ACKNOWLEDGMENTS

In the beginning there was . . .

Renee Nyen, my agent, to whom I dedicate this book, but who must also be acknowledged for her unyielding persistence with this novel. So much of what is on the page is due to her courageous efforts, but also to her willingness to share her truth with me. This was our journey together, and I can't thank her enough.

Thank you to my editor, Jason Kirk, who gave not only Esther her publishing home, but me as well. You are this book's soul mate, and if I may say, mine, too.

A huge thank-you to my publicist, Brittany, and the whole Amazon team, who make publishing a joyride. It takes many hands to bring a book to market, each equally important. From copyediting to cover design, I am so appreciative of your hard work and dedication. Thank you.

Thank you to Anna and Sarah for brainstorming with me all those years ago. Look at where Esther ended up.

Thank you to Angie and Andrea, who offered hope to this book when it was most needed.

Thank you to my husband, Kyle, and our daughters, Drew and Hazel. You are my constant reminder of the numinous. You are my soul mates, my simple loves. Infinity exists in the whole of our family.

Thank you to my parents, Sydney and Russell Schnurr, who showed me that spirituality isn't just found in a church. On a sunny Cleveland day, a poetry reading in the valley with airplanes overhead does the trick.

And to the readers—I'm glad this book found you.

ABOUT THE AUTHOR

Photo © 2018 Kate Testerman Photography

Rebekah Crane is the author of several critically acclaimed young adult novels, including *The Upside of Falling Down*, *The Odds of Loving Grover Cleveland*, *Aspen*—currently being adapted by Life Out Loud Films—and *Playing Nice*. She is a former high school English teacher who found a passion for writing young adult fiction while studying secondary English education at Ohio University. She is a yoga instructor and the mother of two girls. After living and teaching in six different cities, Rebekah finally settled in the foothills of the Rocky Mountains to write novels and work on screenplays. She now spends her days tucked behind a laptop at seventy-five hundred feet, where the altitude only enhances the writing experience. Visit www.rebekahcrane.com, follow the author on Twitter, or like her on Facebook at /authorrebekahcrane.